The Game is Afoot

Mysterious Ink Bookstore Mystery Series: Segue Novella

By Leeann Betts

(c) 2020
ISBN: 978-1-943688-70-8

Published by: PLS Bookworks

Where Publishing Dreams Become Reality

Books By Leeann Betts:

By the Numbers series featuring Carly Turnquist, forensic accountant

No Accounting for Murder

There Was a Crooked Man

Unbalanced

Five and Twenty Blackbirds

Broke, Busted, and Disgusted

Hidden Assets

Petty Cash

A Deadly Dissolution

Silent Partner

In the Money

Missing Deposits

Risk Management

Mysterious Ink Bookstore mystery series featuring Margie Hanson, librarian

Little Grey Cells (releases December 2020)

Counting the Days: a 31-day devotional

In Search of Christmas Past – a novel

By Leeann and Donna:

Nuggets of Writing Gold – articles & essays on writing.

More Nuggets of Writing Gold – more articles & essays on writing

Books by Donna Schlachter:

Mended by God series – bringing healing and
wholeness to your heart and soul
Broken Dreams, Mended Heart
Broken Dreams, Mended Family
Broken Dreams, Mended Marriage

I Do – Again: a devotional for remarrieds

Second Chances and Second Cups: A short story collection.
The Physics of Love
The Mystery of Christmas Inn, Colorado
Christmas Under the Stars
Transformation – a devotional

The Oregon Trail Mysteries series
Kate
A Pink Lady Thanksgiving

Available at Online Retailers and Fine Booksellers:
Quiet Moments Alone with God: a devotional
100 Answers to 100 Questions About Loving Your Husband
Double Jeopardy: a novel about murder, mining, and a mock
marriage
Echoes of the Heart -- The Pony Express Romance
Collection
A Prickly Affair -- Bouquet of Brides Romance Collection
Train Ride to Heartbreak -- Mail Order Brides Romance
Collection
Detours of the Heart – MISSadventure Brides Romance
Collection
The Worst-Kept Secret – Always a Wedding Planner
Collection (releases June 2021)

3

Dedication

First and foremost, to God the Father, Jesus the Son,
And the Holy Spirit.
Without them, no story is worth telling.

To my husband Patrick, my biggest fan.

To my sister-in-law Margie, who I named Carly's first
granddaughter after so many years ago because a
picture of her as a child fit the image of my
fictional Margie perfectly.

Acknowledgements:

Writing a series set in a bookstore is a new endeavor for me, since
I've never worked in or owned a retail business. So I interviewed
Kristyn Niemeyer, the owner of "The Bookworm"
in Gunnison, Colorado, and picked her brain. Thanks, Kristyn.
Any errors are entirely mine.

To determine the value of the rare and valuable books mentioned
in this book, I used two online sites, including Etsy and
Biblio.com. Needless to say, with market fluctuations and other
issues such as condition and provenance, these prices can change
in an instant. If you own rare books, please select a reputable
dealer to value them for you.

Chapter 1

Margie grabbed her ringing cell phone and checked the caller ID. Her Great Aunt Rosella. "Hello?"

"Their voices assault my hearing."

"What are you talking about, Auntie?"

A long sigh. "I already told you." The older woman's voice lowered a notch in both volume and timbre. "Their voices assault my—"

"I heard that. Who are you talking about?"

"The voices."

Margie, newly graduated from Rutgers University with her Masters in Information and Library Sciences, sank back in the lumpy sofa of her off-campus studio apartment. She eyed the cloisonné clock perched beside her recently framed diploma—the clock a graduation gift from her aunt, the diploma the result of six years of diligent study. "Are you hearing voices?"

Three abrupt thumps, and Margie pulled the phone from her ear. What the—? Oh, right. Aunt Rosella often emphasized her displeasure by whacking the nearest tool at hand against the

5

closest hard surface. In this case, her phone likely contacted a table. Or the wall.

"Don't speak to me like I'm a batty old woman. I'm not hearing voices. At least, not in the way your tone implies."

"Sorry. Tell me what's going on."

"What is going on, as you so eloquently put it, is criminal. And that's all I'm going to say about the matter until I speak with you face to face."

Margie unfolded her legs and sat forward. "Are you coming to Maine?" She hadn't seen the older woman in years, although they chatted several times a year by telephone, and her aunt always remembered her on her birthday and at Christmas. And on the occasion of her graduation, of course. "That's great. When?"

"I am not coming to you. You will visit me here in Denver. Immediately, if not sooner."

"But—"

"No buts about it. I have a matter I need you to look into. You have an enquiring mind, child. I've always appreciated that about you."

Margie smiled. "Must have gotten it from you."

"Pshaw. Just because I own a bookstore dedicated to mysteries doesn't mean I can solve them. It simply provides me a business reason to read as much as I like." She chuckled. "But don't tell the tax man."

"My lips are sealed." Margie glanced at the three letters on the coffee table. Job offers. Very good ones, at that. Her dream come true. One at a public library in a small town in Indiana where she'd be librarian, curator, and teacher. The second from a local law firm, where she'd be in charge of the law library and its tomes of precedents and cases. And the third at her alma mater, where she'd be assistant to the chief librarian. The problem was deciding which to accept. "But I can't leave right now. In fact, I have to choose between—"

"Between helping me or abandoning me to the wolves."

"Surely it can't be as bad as that." Spending her days surrounded by mysteries must be affecting her aunt's mental processes. "Perhaps I could come out over Thanksgiving?"

"It will be too late by then." Her aunt sniffed. "Never mind. I suppose there's nothing you can do anyway. You have a good mind for mysteries, as I said. Not as good as your Grandma Carly's, though. She's got a mind like Dame Agatha's. I'll call and see if she's willing to help this old woman."

Margie shook her head, seeing through her aunt's play for sympathy. She leafed through the letters. All three graciously gave her a month to decide, leaving her three more weeks before crunch time. Perhaps a quick dash to Denver for a week or so was in order. Getting away from Augusta might free her mind. Give her time and space to analyze her options. Make the best career choice.

And the mention of her grandmother gave her another idea. "How about if I call Grandma Carly and the two of us visit?"

"Oh, that would be grand. You can stay with me in the apartment over the bookstore. The spare room has two single beds ready and waiting for you."

Interesting how the woman's concerns immediately translated into vacation mode. Possibly things weren't so serious—no, she'd said she'd come. "Grandma can make up for

7

my shortcomings, and you can show us around your beloved Denver."

"Oh, not my *Denver*, dear. My *Edgewater*. I never venture into the Mile High City." Another sniff. "They sell drugs on every corner and call themselves medical dispensaries." A sigh. "Such wickedness."

Margie smiled. No doubt her aunt's little burg also offered marijuana and other previously illicit pleasures, but she'd not spoil the woman's Pollyanna view of *her* Edgewater, a tiny city nestled between Denver, Lakewood, and Wheat Ridge. Situated beside a large lake. The park-like atmosphere with its quaint old-style downtown was exactly the Eden-like surrounding her aunt loved.

Margie scrolled to her calendar app. "I'll call you back to confirm when we'll arrive, and we'll plan to stay a week."

"With your grandmother's help, that should be plenty of time."

"Will somebody meet us at the airport?"

"Yes. My nephew, Arthur. You remember him, don't you?"

Margie's memory cast back to the far-in-the-past family reunions, recalling a weaselly boy with thick eyeglasses and a sarcastic tongue. Hopefully the years had changed him for the better. "Okay. Let me make arrangements, then I'll call you with details."

"Good. And bring the clock I sent you. It's very important. Do you understand?"

"Okay." She glanced up at the item again. After unpacking it yesterday, she hadn't even bothered to wind it up. Just as well, since it would only run out in her suitcase, being a twenty-four-hour mini-version. Decorative, but not very practical. "Anything else?"

"A jar of Maine blueberry jam."

"Got it."

A long silence filled her ear, and she wondered whether her aunt had disconnected. Then a rustling sound. Almost as though Aunt Rosella covered the receiver with a hand. To keep her from hearing a conversation in Edgewater? Or to make certain somebody there didn't hear what she said next?

Neither made sense.

And her aunt's words only added to her confusion.

"The game is afoot."

{ * }

Carly frowned at the words on her computer screen. Writing a mystery was a lot more difficult than solving one. Why, she could have cleared up the FBI's cold case files in the time she'd spent coming up with this story idea, writing the synopsis, and developing the characters. She exhaled. Had she missed a key point in class somewhere along the line?

Flipping flipped back through the binder of class notes and handouts provided no help. Why did returning to college at her age seem a good idea? She should give up this idea of being a novelist. Hard work, long hours, and the fame and fortune scarcer than she'd imagined—she could have stayed working for better pay.

In the back yard, Mike whistled as he worked on yet another project. The man had more ideas on how to improve every system in their house, including the dishwasher, the garbage disposal, and the snow blower, than she had story ideas. He took to retirement like—well, like he was born to it. Her, not so much.

Sure, she didn't miss the cranky customers, or traveling for court appearances. And she absolutely didn't regret not facing defense attorneys trying to tear her expert opinion to shreds. As a forensic accountant, she'd faced her fair share of up-and-comers working hard to make a name for themselves and a buck for their client by hiding assets or doing estranged spouses out of their maintenance and child support.

Routine. That's what she missed the most. Getting up in the morning, knowing what was ahead of her for the day, finalizing a file and closing it. Accomplishing something.

Unlike this never-ending mystery where she had written herself into a corner. She sighed. Back to the class notes and the old drawing board. Dead body. Check. Suspects. Well, she had three, none of them with a great motive. Perhaps she needed to—

Her cell phone rang. She frowned and jabbed the speaker button. "Hello?"

If this was another tele-pest, she'd give him a piece of her mind. Then again, maybe not. She didn't have much to spare.

"Grandma Carly, it's Margie."

Carly turned from the papers and gave her only granddaughter her full attention. "Sweetie, how good to hear your voice. What's up?"

Don and Denise's daughter laughed. "Does something need to be up for me to call my favorite grandmother?"

"Your only grandmother, I might add." Carly picked up the phone, turned off the speaker option, and relaxed into her chair. "Where are you?"

"Still in New Jersey. I have three jobs to decide between, but we can talk about that on the plane."

"Sure, no—wait a minute. What plane?"

Margie giggled. "Figured that would get your attention. If you aren't too busy, can you take a week off and go visit Aunt Rosella with me?"

"Doesn't she live out west somewhere?" Carly's mind raced to fill in the blanks of what she recalled about the woman, related to her son-in-law and not much more than a hazy memory from a Thanksgiving early in her marriage. "Owns a bookstore?"

"Yep, a mystery bookstore. Near Denver. She needs our help."

"*Our* help?" A small groan caught at the back of Carly's throat. Hair stylists and accountants never got time off as far as family and friends are concerned. "Or *your* help? I see where a librarian's skills would come in handy in a bookstore."

"No, she specifically mentioned you. Said you had the best mind for a mystery since Agatha Christie."

"And why would she need that kind of help? Is she in trouble?"

"Don't know. She mentioned voices, told me to bring my graduation present she sent, and then she said something even more strange."

More strange? Hard to believe. "What?"

"She said *the game is afoot*."

"Ah, a reference first to Agatha Christie, and then to Sherlock Holmes. Has she spent too many years in the mystery stacks?"

"I don't know, but I am worried. She sounded serious. Even threatened to call you directly if I didn't agree to come. Like she

11

figured you would do it without my help if need be."

"I wish her confidence in me would translate onto the page."

"Struggling with the novel?"

"Yes. And it's a huge part of my final grade. Not to mention the reason I took this course to begin with. Guaranteed a complete book by the end of the semester."

"Possibly spending time with Aunt Rosella will help sort it out for you. I'm hoping the time away from here will aid me in my decision."

"Good point. A change of venue. I can bring my computer with me. When did you want to go?"

After comparing schedules, the two agreed on dates, leaving in three days. That meant Carly would miss only one class, so first on her list was contacting the professor and getting the notes to keep up. Then book the plane ticket.

Then tell Mike he needed to fend for himself for a few days.

She'd best start with the most difficult task first.

She headed for the back yard.

And Mike.

Chapter 2

Margie strolled down the jet way and into the Denver International Airport, her grandmother close behind. She paused at the gate, her spinner carry-on close to her feet, allowing several impatient passengers to continue to their next destination. "Whew-ee. Some people's children."

Grandma Carly chuckled. "Sounds strange coming from one as young as you."

Margie grinned. "Mom says I'm an old soul."

"That you are." Her grandmother looked around. "I guess we follow the signs."

They alternated between the moving sidewalks and falling into step with other foot traffic heading toward the train that linked the various concourses to the main terminal. Down two levels on the escalator, then they jostled for position as a train eased to a halt.

After settling onto a bench at the rear—or was it the front—of the train car, Grams exhaled. "Well, that flight was better than the one your grandfather and I took to New Mexico several years back."

Margie tilted her head. "Must have been when I was really

small."

"Uh-huh. You were about seven. You probably don't remember."

"I don't." Her head jerked when the train accelerated, and she dug in her heels while gripping her spinner case. "I suspect something must have happened because I vaguely recall all the whispered conversations when you returned." She closed her eyes. "A snowstorm. A dude ranch. Sounds pretty tame."

Grandma Carly shook her head. "Well, before I even got off the plane, I'd solved a murder and seen the two killers escorted off the plane in handcuffs." She sighed. "I wish I'd stopped them."

Margie turned to face her now-greying grandmother. "You solved a murder on the plane?" She giggled. "Oh, just wait until Aunt Rosella hears about this."

"Shh, keep your voice down. People are staring at us."

Instead, Margie straightened her shoulders, thrust her chin out, and made eye contact with the occupants standing nearest them. "My grandmother is the greatest detective alive."

Her grandmother's neck and face turned a most attractive shade of crimson, and Margie stifled a grin.

Payback for all those times she played tricks on me when I was a kid.

She settled back, maintaining her balance by gripping the edge of the bench as the train veered around a sharp corner, the near-black tunnel hurtling toward them at high speeds. This was going to be a great trip. She'd get to know her aunt better, see her grandmother in action, and relax in one of her favorite places in the world: a bookstore.

Three minutes later, and she stepped off the train, swept up

14

with the wave of humanity heading for the escalators that would take them to the arrivals gates. She glanced over her shoulder twice, glad to see her grandmother keeping up with her. The last thing she wanted to do was make a call to Grampa Mike and tell him she lost his wife in the airport.

Most of the passengers veered left for baggage claim, but since she and Grandma Carly packed light, they went directly to passenger pickup. A quick text to her cousin by marriage, Aunt Rosella's nephew Arthur Granger, told him the door number where they waited. Within ten minutes, a silver Lexus pulled up to the curb.

The passenger window rolled down. "Marjie? Carla?"

Margie gritted her teeth at his mispronunciation of her name. Marjie was short for Marjorie, and her name was Margie. For Margaret. She bit her tongue, holding back a lesson in phonetics for him.

And what was it about Carla? How difficult was it to remember two names? Which Aunt Rosella no doubt spoke to him, so it wasn't as if he'd never heard them before.

She sighed.

Some people's children.

So instead of telling him how wrong he was, she pasted on a smile, already knowing she wouldn't like this man, no matter how well acquainted they became. "Yes. I'm Margie, and my Grandma Carly."

Instead of getting out of the car and coming around to load their suitcases, he pressed a button on the dash and the trunk lid hissed up on hydraulic lifters.

"Toss your bags in there, then hop in the back seat. Front

15

seat is my office."

Yep, she didn't like him one little bit.

Which wasn't very Christian of her.

Her mother's gentle smile and equally gentle reproof rang in her ears. *Treat your enemies well so they wonder what makes you different.*

Humph. Well, what made her different right now was she'd do as he instructed, pretend he wasn't a jerk, and enjoy the ride from the airport to her aunt's store. And then she'd avoid this prat as much as possible for the next week. Shouldn't be difficult in a city of over a million.

She hefted her own suitcase and her grandmother's into the spacious trunk, noting that even the spare tire looked freshly waxed. After closing the lid, she slid across the leather seat and buckled herself in, noting her cousin barely waited for her grandmother to tuck her feet inside before stomping on the gas and screeching into the flow of traffic.

"Goodness." Grandma Carly flopped back against the seat, gripping the door handle. "What's the rush?"

Arthur made eye contact via the rearview mirror. "Got an important business meeting downtown at two, and I can't be late."

Margie helped her grandmother snap her seatbelt in place as they took a sharp turn and Arthur slammed on the brakes and the horn simultaneously, muttering something about stupid drivers and perpetual construction. "We could have gotten a cab. Or Aunt Rosella told us about the train system connecting most of the city."

"She was afraid you'd get lost. So she sent me."

Apparently, her aunt hadn't ridden with the man recently, or

16

she'd have decided going missing was preferable to being killed or maimed by his poor driving.

Cars whizzed past in the opposite direction on the highway they merged onto, but Arthur seemed intent on proving his fancy luxury car had more speed and power than anybody else on the road. Weaving in and out of lanes, passing other vehicles on the wrong side, then screeching brakes and squealing tires alternated with his muttering, hand gestures to other drivers, and blatant disregard for the safety of all concerned, marked their journey.

Finally, he entered a curving off-ramp and then eased onto yet another highway. Margie sighed. If they survived this trip, it would be a miracle. She sent up a quick prayer for safety and protection.

And another way to get around the city.

Aunt Rosella said Arthur would drive them wherever they needed to go, but this one thing she was certain of: never again with this man at the wheel.

"Hey, are you listening to me?"

She turned her attention to the obnoxious man in the front seat. "Sorry. The altitude must be clogging my ears."

"I said, she's losing her marbles."

"Who is?"

"Aunt Rosella. You can't believe a thing she says."

Grandma Carly leaned forward. "Really? I talked to her a couple of months ago, and she sounded fine. Made perfect sense."

He waved off her words like a pesky fly at a picnic. "Yeah, well, things have changed. She's hearing voices. Tells me somebody is stealing from her. She's batty, I tell you."

Margie considered the man's words. "Do you still work for her in the store?"

He sniffed. "I don't work *for* her. I work *with* her. We're partners."

This was news. "Really? She started the business, didn't she? Her money? Her idea?"

"Well, ye-e-e-s." A red stain crept up the back of his neck. "But I'm the brain and the brawn that keeps the place running smoothly."

Not what her aunt told her on many occasions. According to Aunt Rosella, he was the fly in the ointment, the ant in the honey. Pesky, hard to get rid of. She'd even offered him money to go start his own business, which he'd taken and blown on some crazy idea for a twenty-four-hour kava bar-laundromat. Lasted just long enough for the ink to dry on the lease.

"So what's this important business meeting you're risking life and limb to attend?"

He chuckled. "I like to keep more than one iron in the fire. You know, not keep all my eggs in one basket and all that sort of thing."

His overuse of clichés hurt her brain. In her experience, people who read widely expanded their vocabulary and rarely resorted to platitudes. He had no excuse. He worked in a bookstore, for goodness' sake.

An off-ramp led to yet another highway, albeit a smaller one with fewer lanes and not so much traffic. They sped past a ramp leading up to Federal Boulevard, then another passing Perry Street, before pulling into the right lane to exit onto Sheridan Boulevard.

18

Arthur caught her eye in the mirror again. "Almost there. Edgewater is just up here. Nice place. A little too small for my liking. Only about five thousand people."

Grandma Carly laughed. "Ten times the size of Bear Cove. Practically a metropolis."

His mouth hardened. "Yeah, well, to each his own. A person should live in a city that reflects their personality and abilities." He shrugged. "Small town. . . "

He didn't complete the sentence. He didn't need to. Her grandmother's eyebrows disappeared beneath her bangs, but she showed much grace in not replying.

Margie smiled. Since coming to faith less than fifteen years ago, her grandmother had changed, leaning on God more and more as time passed. If she and Arthur had met back then, Grandma Carly would have pulled him through a knot hole and thought nothing of it.

The man was indeed lucky.

A right turn onto Sheridan, up over a hill with houses and apartment buildings crowding the street, then down toward a shopping area. A large lake to the right hosted speed boats and water skiers, with a walking path crowded with folks pushing strollers or walking dogs. And sometimes both.

Arthur slowed at a light, then darted across the intersection on the yellow-turned-red. Margie shook her head, amazed that the man didn't get more tickets for speeding, reckless driving, and running lights. Or all three.

And if there was a violation for being obnoxious, they should rename it in his honor.

Margie stared out the car window at the sight before her.

19

Like an old-timey old-fashioned town, Edgewater lay all around her. Buildings from the latter part of the 19th and early years of the 20th centuries, the year of their construction boasting their endurance, lined both sides of 25th Avenue.

About halfway down the street, he pulled into a small parking lot beside the bookstore which occupied the street level of an old house. Aunt Rosella lived upstairs so she was close to her favorite friends, as she called her books.

Arthur shut off the car and hopped out, heading for a side door. Margie glared at him. His mother certainly didn't raise a gentleman. Or if she had, he'd acquired a number of bad habits on his own.

She quirked her chin toward the store. "Grandma, let's go in first. We can bring our bags once we are ready to settle in."

"Good idea."

She dug into her carry-on for the hostess gift she'd brought. Unable to bring more than a one-ounce container on the plane, she'd purchased a variety pack at the airport of purportedly authentic jams and jellies from her home state. Thankfully, there were two kinds that contained blueberries. Maine berries, she wasn't certain.

The two exited the car and followed Arthur inside.

But when Margie pushed the door open, it met with an immovable object. "Arthur, we can't get in. Can you help?"

His face appeared in the small opening. "Um, um—" He glanced over his shoulder. "She—she—"

Margie pushed the door, forcing him to step out of the way. "What is going on? Why can't we come in? Where is Aunt Rosella?"

20

She followed his line of sight. Through the bookstore. Into a hallway. That led to a staircase.

At the bottom was a bag of laundry.

Or a rolled-up carpet.

Or a large stuffed animal.

Grandma Carly pressed in from behind. "Can I come in too? I'm dying to see the store. And to see Rosella—"

Her words hung in the air, pointing like fingers of accusation. The gift in Margie's hand weighed as heavy as a ship's anchor, threatening to fall to the floor and crash through.

Along with her heart.

Not dirty clothes. Not floor covering. Not a giant teddy bear.

{*}

Carly stared at the lump. Was it only an hour ago when she joked foolishly with Margie about no murder this far into their trip?

What had she been thinking?

Margie made a motion as if to step closer, but Carly barred her passage. "Wait. We don't want to contaminate what might be a crime scene."

Arthur, his haughty manner vanished along with most of the color in his previously florid face, gawked at her. "Crime scene?" He gestured up the stairs. "It's obvious what happened. She tripped and fell down the stairs. I've been telling her she should move into an apartment where she'd be safer. Would she listen to me?" He shook his head. "She wouldn't. She must be near her babies, as she called them." He snorted. "Books."

Carly turned her attention to the man. "Seems a strange comment coming from somebody whose livelihood depends on those books."

21

Another snort. "I don't have to work here. I'm not a mere clerk. I have—"

She turned away, unable to look at the detestable man one more minute. "I know. Irons in the fire."

She circled Rosella's body, noting the open eyes, slack hands, unnatural twist in the neck. Sneakers with hook-and-loop fasteners. No shoelaces to trip in. Capri pants. No long skirt to catch under a foot.

Around the far side, she tested the handrail. Sturdy. Nothing loose. A glance up the staircase showed bare wood. No carpet. No runner.

No reason to fall in a place the woman passed at least twice every day.

For a woman nearing eighty, there were plenty of other reasons to fall. A moment of vertigo. A joint giving out. Familiarity breeding contempt leading to hurry or carelessness.

And, while she didn't want to consider the who or the why, there was always murder. A push. A shove. A wire strung across a step. A sedative that hadn't worn off. A blow to the back of the head.

She had more questions than answers.

She turned toward Arthur, not quite meeting his gaze. There was something slippery and—slimy, yes, that was the word—about the man. "Call the police."

"Yes."

Carly jumped at a tap on the door to the bookstore. Goodness, had Arthur already summoned the law? She wove a path through the stacks and displays and peered through the glass. "It's a woman."

"With an outlandish wig?"

Carly smiled. Arthur had pegged their visitor perfectly. Coiffed in a shoulder-length blonde composition that would have made several big-name country singers jealous, the elderly woman looked a contender for a Dolly Parton-lookalike contest. "Yes."

"Let her in. It's Bernadette. She owns the wig store down the street. She and my aunt were best friends."

Were being the operative word. She'd follow up on that later. *Were* because Rosella was dead, or *were* because they'd had a falling out?

She turned the deadbolt, but before she planted her foot to bar the woman's entry, the octogenarian pushed her way in.

"What's wrong?" Bernadette glanced around, eyes wide. "I called her, but she didn't answer her phone."

Carly stepped out from behind the door and introduced herself. "My granddaughter and I are here to visit Rosella. Do you call her often?"

"She checks in with me every night ever since my husband passed away three years ago. And I call her every morning to make certain she doesn't sleep in. She hates opening the shop even a minute late."

"I'm afraid there's been an accident."

When Arthur entered the shop, Bernadette stiffened and glared at him, pointing a finger in his direction. "Finally killed her, did you? Well, she'll have the last laugh. She changed her will last month and left everything to me."

Arthur stepped closer, his five-six frame towering over the wig lady's. Color returned to his face. "She wouldn't do that. She told me she had an appointment this week. I depended—" He

23

clamped his mouth shut and turned his gaze toward the door. "It's like Grand Central Station here. Look who else turned up at the wake."

A lanky man with grey hair cut short stepped in through the door. "Is somebody throwing a party? My invitation must be in the mail." He smiled and held out a hand to Carly. "Ted Bloom."

She returned the gesture and introduced herself. "Let me guess. You're a florist."

He grinned. "No, but perhaps I should consider that. It would make for a fun tagline." He glanced at the other occupants then closed the door. "And you must be Margie, Rosella's great-niece."

Margie set a paper bag on the counter and nodded. "Yes. She mentioned you a time or two. Said you were great friends."

He tilted his head in question. "Were? That sounds ominous." He turned to Bernadette. "What brings you out this morning?"

"She didn't answer when I called this morning."

He chuckled. "Slept in, no doubt."

The wig lady shook her head. "No. Something has happened. They said so."

Being taller, Ted had a practically unobstructed view of the hallway outside the shop walls. "What's that at the bottom of the—" His eyes widened. "No. Let me see."

Carly touched his forearm. "Not until we have called the police."

He stared down at her. "You haven't done that yet? What if she's still alive? Unconscious. Call the paramedics. They might be able to save her."

Carly gripped his arm, sinewy but muscular under his long-sleeved shirt. "She's gone. I'm sorry."

Bernadette wailed, a long, drawn-out howl reminiscent of a wolf call, then she collapsed into a high-back chair near the door. "Oh, my poor, poor Rosella."

A lump rose in Carly's throat, threatening to cut off her breathing. Although she wasn't close with Rosella, the unjust, unlawful, too-soon death of another riled her. She sighed. "We must call the police."

Ted pulled his cell phone from a shirt pocket. "Before you do, I'm calling Rosella's lawyer."

Strange choice. Unless he thought *he* needed a lawyer.

As if hearing her thoughts, he punched a number and held the phone to his ear. "Rosella promised she'd leave the store to me, and I want to be certain my successor rights are followed." He grunted then disconnected. "Busy."

Arthur snorted. Appeared his pet method of expressing what he felt. "She left it to me."

Bernadette lifted her head, apparently recovered enough to take part in the conversation. "No, she left everything to me. I was her only staunch friend, not after her for what she had. Or what she'd give."

Carly turned, her head fairly swimming with potential suspects. Each of these three people believed they were heir to Rosella's estate. Was that understanding enough to propel one of them to murder, if that's what this was?

At a second tap on the door, she turned again. Arthur said the population of Edgewater was in the neighborhood of five thousand folks, and it seemed each one intended to visit the store today.

A svelte red-head cupped her hands around her eyes and peered in. Carly sighed. Might as well see what this one wanted.

She opened the door. "Yes?"

"Is everything all right?"

"And you are?"

"Ginger. I own the salon next door." She stepped inside. "Oh, hello Bernadette. Ted. Arthur."

Margie, shoulders slumped, pasted on a smile. "I'm—"

"Margie. Rosella's been so excited about your visit. She told me all about it a few days ago when she came in for a shampoo and set." She turned to Carly. "And you must be Carly."

"I am. There's been an accident."

"Is Rosella okay? She doesn't like hospitals, you know."

There were probably a lot of things about to happen that the older woman wouldn't approve of. Including being hauled out on a stretcher. The autopsy. Carly shivered. "Why did you want to see her?"

"My shop is next door. Just before nine, I saw somebody ring the doorbell to the shop. It rings upstairs, you know."

This was information she might use. "Did you recognize the person?"

Ginger shook her head. "No."

"Male or female?"

"Couldn't tell. Wore pants, running shoes, baggy sweatshirt. Curly hair covering the ears. Hat pulled low. Sunglasses." She held a hand a few inches shorter than her own five-eight or so. "About this tall."

The description impressed Carly. "Then what?"

Ginger shrugged. "I guess Rosella let her in, because the door opened, and I lost sight of them."

Margie's brow pulled down. "Nine? That's before normal business hours for Aunt Rosella, isn't it?"

Ted nodded. "Yes, but sometimes she made appointments for special customers. Or if she had a collector looking for a particular book. Even somebody dropping off books."

Interesting business model. "So Rosella bought books from individuals?"

He crossed his arms over his chest. "Individuals. Stores going out of business. Thrift stores trying to move inventory. Publishers. Folks even gave her books. She'd take anything and everything, sort through the lot, keep what she wanted, and cycle the rest back through libraries, thrift stores, nursing homes."

Carly envisioned the boxes of books stored in her basement in Bear Cove. She'd already given so many to the library that they told her to stop bringing them in. She meant to donate them to the Riverdale library where her daughter and family lived, but never remembered to put them in the car.

Sounded like Rosella had a great system.

Bernadette joined their conversation circle. "Occasionally she'd come across a rare find that was worth a lot of money. Last year she sold a first edition Poe for several thousand dollars." She clasped her hands together, tying her fingers into knots. "Not that she'd tell me exactly how much, of course."

Arthur sniffed this time. Perhaps a lesser reaction. "She knew little to nothing about valuable books. I found that one in a box from an estate sale and pointed it out to her. But did she give me so much as a finder's fee? No. She said I'd see my commission

27

when she died." He looked around. "None of you had better be telling the truth about her will. I'm her blood. I will fight the will in court if need be."

The three potential heirs circled each other, although they didn't actually move. If they'd been dogs, their ruffs would have bristled and their lips would have pulled back, baring their teeth.

And Carly would be running for a bucket of water.

But they weren't canines. They were actual people. Apparently hoodwinked by sweet Rosella.

Funny how even the nicest of people so easily made enemies.

Chapter 3

Margie perched on the stool behind the bookstore cash register, her hostess gift mocking her. She tucked it on the shelf beneath the display case. Her head swam as she struggled to keep up with the multiple conversations going on around her. Near the New Books section, Arthur and Ginger kept up a lively banter—or rather, gossip—about who was seeing whom amongst the business owners of the downtown section.

In the hallway, her grandmother and the police detective discussed the scene. The responding officer, a boy barely out of his teens, it seemed, had backed away from the body and scurried back to his patrol car in record time. The detective showed up a leisurely twenty minutes after that, taking control of the investigation with his badge and his baritone voice.

Relaxing in the easy chairs in the reading area, Ted and Bernadette still argued over who was the beneficiary.

She couldn't take much more of this.

And she didn't have to.

She crossed the store that felt as packed with bodies—no, best not to use that term, even in her thoughts—with customers as if this were a sale day, and stood before the maintenance man and the fake hair lady. "There is one way to resolve this argument, you know."

Bernadette looked up at her, batting her also-fake eyelashes like a hummingbird's wings. And almost the same size, too. "And how is that?"

"Call her attorney." Margie pulled her phone from her back pocket. "What's his number?"

Ted shifted in the chair. "I don't think—"

She opened her browser app. "I'm not asking you to think. You just called him."

Ted clamped his mouth shut, so Bernadette answered. "Robert Lowe."

Margie looked up from her cell. "Like the actor?"

"Huh?"

Now those eyelashes went into turbo-boost.

"Rob Lowe. The hunky actor."

Bernadette somehow pumped the dumb-yet-innocent look up another two notches. "I don't know. He isn't an actor. Actors have lots of money. The good ones, anyway. And I always figured lawyers did, too. But not Robert Lowe. He was always teasing Rosella that when she died, all his money problems would go away."

Didn't sound much like a topic to joke about. "Do you know why he needed money?"

The wig vendor shrugged. "Rosella never said. Although she made a comment once about not honoring his marriage bed and sharing those rights with another woman." She sniffed. "I can't believe anything she said to me. She lied to me about my inheritance."

Was her great-aunt so lonely and bereft of friends she

30

needed to promise these people money to keep them around? Margie shrugged. Her aunt she knew. These two were strangers. Perhaps they were lying to her. Talking to them was like trying to carry on a conversation with the three stooges—even though there were only two of them. "No matter. I'll track him down."

She returned to the stool and, using speech-to-text, asked the app for the attorney's name. When the information popped up on the screen, she pressed the call symbol, and within minutes was talking to the man himself.

"Thank you, that's interesting information. I'll get in touch with you in a day or so. Yes, it was a shock. Yes, the police are here now. I'll give them your name and number. Goodbye."

She disconnected the call and returned to where Ted and Bernadette were now discussing their individual plans on running their inheritance. At complete odds with each other, of course. She smiled and cleared her throat, waiting until they quieted. "I just talked to Aunt Rosella's attorney. He said she changed her will last week. Signed it the next day, so it's all legal and complete."

Ted straightened in the chair. "And?"

"And you don't have to worry about getting rid of these junky books so you can open a small appliance repair store."

Bernadette hooted. "See, I told you she wouldn't forget about me." The woman waved her arms around. "I can see it now. I'll clear out those dusty shelves, rip up this ratty carpet, and—"

Margie shook her head. "Save the talk. She didn't leave it to you, either."

"What?" The wig lady jumped to her feet. "She promised."

31

She glared across the room where Arthur loomed over the perky stylist. "Don't tell me she left it to that freeloader."

"No. She left it to me."

{*}

Carly gritted her teeth at Detective Ed Hogan's condescending attitude. "But Detective—"

The Columbo lookalike, right down to his rumpled overcoat and unkempt hair, was not a man to trifle with, apparently. "No, Mrs. Turnquist. It's like I said. She fell down the stairs. It was an accident."

"Well, yes, I can see why you might think that. And there isn't much doubt that she fell down the stairs, as you said. But you ought to—"

"No, ma'am. See, this is how I work. I investigate. Amateurs stay out of my way." He nodded to a woman wearing white overalls. "Doc Heather, our coroner. TOD?"

The doctor straightened, checked the liver probe, and closed her eyes a moment. "Died between six and ten."

Margie's breath caught in her throat. "Somebody visited her just before nine. Ginger saw them."

Carly nodded. "We arrived just before ten, and she was cool then."

Doc Heather narrowed her eyes. "You touched the body?"

"Just to check for a pulse."

"Are you medical?"

Carly shook her head. "No. I was a forensic accountant. Now I'm retired and I write mysteries."

Detective Hogan rolled his eyes. "Should'a known. An amateur."

"Just a minute, Detective. You're right. I'm not a trained medical professional. And I'm not law enforcement. But I was an expert witness on all things pertaining to accounting for many years. And I assisted in several murder cases, too."

Another eye roll. "Even worse. I bet you watch all the forensic shows, right? Expect DNA results in twenty-two minutes. Fingerprints lifted from a hair. You probably like to gather all the suspects and do a Miss Marple on them, too." He nodded to the coroner. "If you're done, you can take her away."

Carly sighed. "So you're going with natural causes?"

The coroner shook her head. "No, I don't make a conclusion and look for evidence that fits my theory. I'll do a full autopsy. Right now it's a suspicious death."

"Rosella was in good health. There was no reason for her to fall."

Hogan stepped closer. "I don't need help from amateurs." He turned to the coroner. "Looks like natural causes to me."

"We'll see, but you're probably right."

Carly groaned. Now there were two against her one.

Still, she'd been in tougher situations before.

And this time, she had help. Her granddaughter has a mind like a steel trap, especially for solving mysteries.

Rosella wasn't here to speak for herself, so she and Margie would be the dear woman's spokespersons.

They would uncover the truth.

{*}

Margie carried a tea tray into Aunt Rosella's—no, now it was her—living room and set it on the coffee table. "Shall I pour?"

Grams, a wooly blanket over her knees, nodded. "Please do.

33

I can't move yet."

She lifted the teapot and poured Earl Grey into the dainty china cups. "So like Aunt Rosella to have all the finer things in life, isn't it?" She handed the cup and saucer to her grandmother. "I wish I'd known her better."

"Me, too." Her grandma, looking a little the worse for wear, blew on the hot beverage before sipping. "Oh, that's good." She sank back into the sofa. "I haven't seen her for years, although we exchanged Christmas letters. And your mother kept me up on the wild and crazy adventure Rosella called life."

Margie chuckled. "I remember hearing stories about her when I was a kid. The things she did seemed too fantastical. I was sure Mom and Dad were making up stories to keep me entertained. But then we came here for a visit when I was about ten, and I saw they weren't telling me half of what she'd done. It's when I really and truly fell in love with books, wandering through the stacks downstairs. Thinking how wonderful it would be to own all those books."

"She loved them all, you know, like old friends. Told me once she didn't sell them. She merely adopted them to a new home for a small fee."

Margie sipped her own brew. "I like that." She glanced around the room. "I can't believe it's all mine now. I mean, why would she leave me a bookstore halfway across the country?"

"She knew exactly what she was doing. I can't imagine why any of those three leeches thought she'd entrust her baby to either one of them."

She shuddered. "I know. While you were talking with the detective, Ted and Bernadette were arguing over who had the best idea for tossing the books and starting a new business." Another shiver. "Poor Aunt Rosella would be like a rotisserie chicken, spinning in her grave if that ever happened."

"You have some big decisions to make."

"Even before I came here, I already did. I have three job offers for three dream jobs." Another look around the area, built-in bookcases crammed with all manners of mystery novels, on all walls. "Yet, this place is growing on me."

"And you took business courses, didn't you?"

"Two. I had several choices, such as something useless like Atlantic Folklore or Medieval Storytelling, but decided the accounting gene from you had a hold on me. If I'm going to run a business, some of that information will come in handy."

"And I'm happy to help, too. Give advice. I can go over whatever records we find and let you know the financial condition."

"That would be great, but I didn't bring you here to work."

Grandma Carly laughed. "You know me. Numbers are my friends."

When Margie's cell rang, she set her tea aside and answered. "Hi, Detective Hogan. Yes, let me put the phone on speaker so she can hear, too."

"Hello, Mrs. Turnquist. The autopsy is completed, and the doc found something interesting. An injection site on the back of her arm just above the elbow. Tests show a long-lasting insulin injection immediately prior to death. There are bruises on the back of her arms, too, suggesting somebody gripped her from behind."

Grandma gasped. "So the case remains open?"

"For now. But I'm thinking this was a break-in. Her nephew told us of several rare and valuable books that were in the glass case where the cash register sits. At least one isn't there now."

Margie's brow furrowed. "That makes little sense."

"Sure it does. She hears a noise downstairs. Goes down to investigate. Sees an intruder. Runs upstairs to call the police. The thief chases her, injects the insulin, then pushes her down the stairs. Takes the books and leaves."

No, it didn't make sense at all. "What self-respecting burglar comes armed with insulin? Why didn't she use the bookstore phone to call the police? How did the burglar get in leaving no trace? The door to the store wasn't forced, and neither was the one we entered off the parking lot."

Papers rustled in the detective's office. "Well, I'm sure we'll get the answers to all those questions. Was the thief was a diabetic who carried his insulin with him at all times? Possibly she thought she could sneak back upstairs without him knowing she was there. And perhaps she'd forgotten to lock a door. Old people do that, you know. Forget things."

"But—" Margie's CALLER ID showed that Aunt Rosella's attorney was calling. "Thank you, Detective. Please keep us updated."

"I shall."

She swiped over to answer Mr. Lowe's call. "I'm putting you on speaker phone so my grandmother can hear, too." Another tap. "Go ahead."

"Hello, ladies. I was hoping to set up an appointment with you, Margie, for tomorrow afternoon to go over your great-aunt's will."

36

"That would be fine. What time?"

"How about three?" A pause. "And Margie?"

"Yes?"

"I've had a call from the detective in charge of the case. I gave him a summary of Rosella's will. And he told me about your conversations with him. Particularly Mrs. Turnquist's chat."

"And?"

"I suggest you step aside and let the professionals do their jobs. That would be the detective. Me. It's what we get paid the big bucks for." He chuckled. "I have you scheduled for three tomorrow."

Margie opened her calendar app and made a note. "Perfect. See you then."

"Good. As her executor, I can assure you I will move this through probate quickly and efficiently."

"Thank you." She disconnected the call. "Interesting. Sounds like he's motivated to get this done as soon as possible." She set the phone aside. "I didn't particularly like his ill-concealed warning to stay out of the investigation."

Grandma Carly nodded. "The detective said as much to me, too." She finished her tea. "It's in his best interests, you know. Executors are paid a percentage of the value of the estate. I don't know how much Rosella was worth, but judging by this building, I'd say quite a bit."

"All the more reason to see Mr. Lowe as soon as possible. Bernadette made a comment about him always needing money. I just put it off to her disappointment in not being named in the will."

Grandma Carly nodded. "Rosella was a lot smarter than folks

37

gave her credit for. Which might have gotten her killed."

Chapter 4

Margie carried her coffee cup into the living room the next morning and curled up on the sofa. Already the sun was high in the sky, and the weather app on her cell told her the temperature was in the mid-seventies, with low eighties forecast for the high. She sighed. Colorado definitely had nicer weather than Maine, at least this time of the year. Not to mention the lower humidity.

Still, despite inheriting the bookstore, she wasn't certain she wanted to live here indefinitely. There were other considerations, including being so far from family. And although Edgewater was small, Denver, with its population of more than two million, was practically next door.

She sipped her coffee. Did she really want to live in a major metropolis? She was more of a small-town girl.

And what of those three job offers awaiting her decision? Owning a bookstore was markedly different from spending her days in a library or a law firm.

Grandma Carly padded into the room, stretching and yawning. "Oh, good. Coffee is on." She held up a hand and headed for the kitchen. "I don't even want to think until I've had my first jolt of java."

Margie smiled and settled into the overstuffed sofa, letting her eyes roam the comfortable room. Books, books, everywhere. She suspected there were more books stored in nooks and crannies throughout the apartment, the store, and even the attic.

Her grandmother pit-patted into the room and sat in a leather recliner, raising her feet. "This is the life."

Margie laughed. "Sure. For a few days. And then you'd be climbing the walls. One of your stories would race through your head, and you'd need to get it into your computer."

"You know me too well."

"Enough to know you might enjoy this now. Particularly after the day we put in getting here and finding Aunt Rosella and all that entailed."

"True."

"I slept like a log. How about you?"

"I did once I got used to hearing the traffic and sirens outside my window."

Margie sat forward. "Noisy compared to home?"

"No worries. Took me about a half hour, and I was out like a light." She tasted her coffee. "Oh, that is good."

"What about that detective?"

Her grandmother grunted. "Like most law enforcement. They don't want anybody upsetting their routine."

"I'm glad you pushed back a little yesterday. Otherwise he might have convinced the coroner it was a simple accident."

Grams shook her head. "It might appear that way, but they are both sharp cookies. Neither really believed she merely fell down the stairs."

"So why would they tell us different?"

"For the simple reason they don't want us getting involved."

Her grandmother chuckled. "They hate all the real life cop and crime shows. Like he said, everything neatly wrapped up in less than an hour, including commercial breaks. Gives folks unrealistic expectations about what the police and labs can accomplish."

"I guess." Margie inhaled the heady smell of her coffee, enjoying the taste on the back of her tongue as much as when she actually drank it. "So what are we going to do?"

Her grandmother blinked several times. "Do? Why should we do anything?"

"Because neither of us are prone to sitting around and waiting for somebody else to come up with the answers. I'd like to know why Aunt Rosella asked us to come here. Why she thought she needed our help." Tears blurred her vision. Every time she remembered the older woman, her heart ached with the injustice of her untimely death. She sniffled. "And why was the clock important? I'd just received it. But she told me to be certain to bring it with me."

"Perhaps she had a story about it she wanted to share."

Margie shook her head. "I don't think so." She stood. "I'm going to shower, then we'll get something to eat, and then we need to go talk to people."

"Good idea. I'll cook, since I showered last night. And who should we talk to first?"

"Let's start with Arthur. Seems he was the most likely to expect to inherit, and perhaps the one who'd be most interested in preventing her from changing her will."

"And he looked surprised to learn she'd changed her will last week. He thought she was seeing the attorney this week. Which would give him a motive to kill her before that. Particularly if she

41

told him the previous will left everything to him."

Margie set her cup on the coffee table. "And then there's Bernadette. She sounded peeved at the news about the will. And a disguise would be simple."

"Sounds like we have a plan." Grams sighed then stood. "Are you tired? My legs don't seem to want to hold me up."

"A little. It's the altitude. Drink lots of water. That's what the guide books say. And limit the caffeine."

Her grandmother headed for the kitchen. "Sound like Mike wrote that drivel. Next you'll tell me chocolate is off my list for the duration of my stay here in the Mile High City."

"I wouldn't endanger life and limb. See you in fifteen minutes."

As Margie headed for the shower, she pondered the unanswered questions floating around in her head, fighting for space. Maybe mystery-solving wasn't her thing.

Then again, Grandma Carly said different. And Aunt Rosella seemed to believe so, too.

Feeling like Watson to Conan Doyle's Holmes, she prayed the hot water would wash away the cobwebs in her brain and the aches in her muscles.

They had a murder to solve.

{*}

Carly led the way down the stairs and into the bookstore where Arthur, nattily attired in a suit and tie, perched on the stool behind the register, reading a magazine featuring old houses.

Hmph. Not even a book. He surely didn't seem interested in promoting the store. What if a customer came in and saw him?

Rosella's nephew looked up when she drew near. He set the

magazine aside, a scowl marring his soft but handsome face. "What do you want?"

Margie came around her and placed her hands on the counter. "To talk to you."

He turned his attention to his distantly related cousin. "About what?"

"Your customer service skills. Or rather, your lack of."

He glanced around the store. "There are no customers."

"Perhaps that is the point?" She turned to face the door. "What do they see when they come in? A man reading a magazine." She turned back. "Which this store doesn't even sell."

"Nobody will come in. Aunt Rosella was the personality behind this store."

Margie nodded. "Exactly. And now we are the new personalities. So we must try harder to make this a refuge for readers. A monastery for mystery lovers. A sanctuary for Sherlock fans, and a preserve for Poe readers."

"You are as batty as she was."

Carly stepped closer. "She's not, and Rosella wasn't, either." She peered at him. "Saying otherwise doesn't make it true."

"Fine." He shoved the magazine beneath the counter. "As the new *owner*, what do you want me to do?"

Margie offered him a tiny smile. "I'd like you to address the three boxes of books lined up against that wall. Are they coming in or going out?"

"In. But that will take hours."

"Good. We have a few errands to run. When we get back, have those double-checked for value, priced, entered into the inventory, and shelved. And then we can start on the next thing."

His brow pulled down, narrowing his eyes to slits. "You won't get away with this, you know."

"Get away with what?"

"I'm her real beneficiary. She said so. She paid me a pittance all these years, saying I'd get what was due me she died."

Sounded like something Rosella would say.

Carly strolled over to the boxes of books Margie mentioned, picking up an old volume sitting on top. "Where did these come from?"

"An estate sale Aunt Rosella went to a couple of weeks ago."

"Interesting." Carly flipped to the title page. A 1943 first edition, first printing of a Raymond Chandler mystery. Probably worth quite a bit, even with the faded dust jacket. She returned the book to its place. "I could get lost in a place like this."

He grunted. "Yeah, well, I tried to talk her into expanding the genres. Attract more customers. Younger people don't read mysteries. That's just for old fogies."

Carly turned and cleared her throat. "A book that is both fun to read and intellectually stimulating will never go out of style." She pulled out her cell phone and entered the author and title. Wow. A similar copy on an online selling platform sold for almost three thousand dollars. "No matter what the age of the reader."

"Whatever." He removed his jacket and hung it on the back of the stool. "I'll send you the cleaning bill for my shirt and pants."

"No need. If you don't want your clothes dirtied, wear something else. Suit and tie not required."

"I have a business—"

Margie's eyebrows arched. "Another business meeting?" She tsk-tsked. "Seems you're out of the shop more than you're here. Aren't you on the schedule for the next few days?"

"Well, yes. But Aunt Rosella—"

"Loved this place so much she was likely always here, right?"

He nodded, eyes staring at the floor.

"Well, I love books, too, but I'm not paying you for time you're not actually here. Doing something. And there is plenty to do. Clear?"

He glared at her, his mouth a straight line. "Crystal." He smirked then pulled a sheet of paper from his jacket pocket. "And perhaps this will make our relationship even more unequivocal." He held the item toward her. "Go ahead. Look at it."

Margie unfolded the document, scanned it, and gasped. "But this can't be. The attorney has the most recent will. Changed last week. Signed by Aunt Rosella."

"Like I said, batty. She went to all that trouble and expense, then turned around and had me write another for her. Leaving everything to me. Dated just three days ago." He tapped the bottom of the page. "And her signature. All legal."

"The lawyer will need to see this. To confirm it's not a forgery."

He snatched the will out of her hands. "No way. This doesn't go out of my sight. It would be just like you to destroy it and deny you ever saw it."

Her granddaughter's shoulders stiffened. "My pastor says that whatever another accuses me of, it's exactly what they'd do. Or are doing."

"Oh, you're one of those goody-two-shoes, are you? Bible thumper?" His top lip curled in a sneer. "Born again do-gooders? Well, you might be all of those things. But you aren't Aunt Rosella's beneficiary."

Grandma Carly sidled closer again. "Why didn't you bring this up yesterday when we talked about the will? In fact, you seemed most surprised that Rosella saw her attorney last week."

"I—I forgot about it."

She shook her head. "Doesn't seem logical to me, to forget a document that would contradict one in her lawyer's hands. Sounds more like you fabricated this overnight, producing it now to cast aspersions on my granddaughter and her rights of inheritance."

He stepped back, the will gripped in his hand. "Say what you like. I'll sue you for libel."

Margie shook her head. "It's slander, not libel."

"What?"

"Never mind. Process those books by the time I get back, or you'll be looking for another job. And we'll let the lawyers sort out this business of a subsequent will. For now, I'm the owner. Mr. Lowe said so. And he's proceeding through probate, so if you really have a claim on the estate, you'd best get to it." She turned and led the way to the front door, pausing before exiting. "After you've finished your work. If you're going to contest the will, do it on your own time."

On the street, Carly exhaled and chuckled. "You are one tough cookie."

"He really got my dander up." Margie looked up and down the street. "Where to next?"

"Bernadette. I want to check out her offerings to see if perhaps she used one of her own wigs to disguise herself." She laid a hand on Margie's arm. "And when we go back, check to make sure that book made it into inventory at the right price."

"Did she disinherit him because he was stealing from her?"

"Possibly. In my experience, staying out of prison and gaining or keeping money are two excellent reasons for murder."

{*}

Margie drew a deep breath before stepping into the wig store. A musty smell tickled her nose, and she stifled a sneeze. The bell over the door tinkled, and the curtain separating the retail area from the back rustled.

"Be right with you."

Her grandmother strolled around the store, pointing out several outrageous headpieces before pulling one particularly attractive piece from its mannequin head and tugging it into place. She checked her image in the mirror. "Hmm, this one is nice. Might make a pleasant change." She turned around. "What do you think?"

"I like it. But why not have your own hair styled in the same manner?"

"This one's short. Darker than my hair. A little curl over the ears and at the back of the neck." She adjusted the piece. "This one would be nice for going out somewhere special."

Margie laughed. "Such as? The fish and chip store for lunch?"

"Good point." Grams set the wig back on its stand. "It feels like real hair."

Bernadette breezed into the retail area. "And it is. All of my best pieces are real hair. They do everything real hair does except grow. You can wash them, curl them, cut them if you dare." She shuddered. "Although why you'd want to change the style, I don't know."

Margie nodded. "I remember a lady in our town who had cancer. She had several wigs, and she sent them in for cleaning occasionally."

The store owner's smile slipped. "Yes, that is a disadvantage to the synthetic headpieces. Although washing at home is possible, we recommend sending them in every couple of months for a thorough treatment."

Time to get this unofficial interview moving. "How is the wig business these days?"

The woman straightened to her full height of just over five feet. "As with most industries, there are difficulties. We're in a rise in popularity again. Buying options are greater, too. So much online these days. But I get my fair share of customers who want that personal touch. Who like to try the piece on before buying."

Grandma Carly glanced back at the wig she'd tried on. "That's good to know." She moved on to the next display, platinum blondes of all lengths and volume. Then she paused and turned back. "You know, that one reminds me of something, but for the life of me, I can't think what. Or who."

What was she up to now? It wasn't like her grandmother to belabor a point unless she was on to something. Margie studied the piece. So where had they talked about short, curly hair?

Right. The person who entered the bookstore the morning Aunt Rosella died. Could have been a disguise. Easiest thing in the world for somebody to don a wig and baggy clothes to cloud identification of gender and size.

She turned to Bernadette, whose face had lost all its color. "Don't you hate it when you can't remember something?" She chuckled. "Happens to me, too, so it's not age-related, Grandma."

Her grandmother tossed her a half-smile. "That's good to hear." She pointed to a grouping of chairs near the rear of the retail area. "Can we sit? My feet are killing me. Still not used to the altitude, I guess."

Another ploy to put Bernadette off her game.

The wig seller's smile didn't quite make it to her eyes, but she led the way and gestured for them to take their choice of seating. "So, what's new with poor Rosella's unfortunate accident?"

Margie crossed one leg over the other and sat back, shrugging the kinks from her shoulders. "Well, it wasn't an accident. The coroner found an injection site and evidence of insulin."

Bernadette gasped. "She didn't tell me she was a diabetic. Such a nasty disease, you know."

Grandma Carly leaned forward. "Medicine has made great strides in that direction."

"Not enough. My husband was diabetic. It's what killed him, finally, you know. It ate away at him a bit at a time. Neuropathy of the feet. Amputation. Organ failure. Congestive heart failure." She wrapped her arms around herself. "Too cruel. And often lingering. Took every dime to care for him."

Margie's heart softened for the woman's pain, but they still had to sort this out mystery. "Well, Aunt Rosella wasn't a diabetic. Which makes the police think this wasn't an accident but

49

murder. Somebody killed her then pushed her down the stairs to disguise the murder."

"That's terrible. Who would do such a thing?"

Grams shrugged. "Somebody she let into her house outside business hours. Somebody she trusted to turn her back on them."

Bernadette's mouth turned down. "Why do you say that?"

"The killer stabbed her in the back of the arm. Then grabbed her and threw down the stairs like a bag of trash."

The wig-lady's hand flew to her throat, toying with a small crucifix dangling there. "No, that sounds more like the work of a madman. Surely none of her friends would do that."

Margie peered at her. Was her distress genuine? Or was guilt eating at her? As a Catholic, the woman recognized the difference between right and wrong. Understood what the Church said about murder. "Changing the subject, Aunt Rosella told me she heard voices. Did she mention anything like that to you?"

Bernadette's eyebrows, penciled-in and already high on her forehead, disappeared beneath the bangs of her current wig choice. "No. Never. Strange she wouldn't. We shared many confidences." She paused. "Then again. . . "

Grandma Carly tilted her head in question. "Then again what?"

"Arthur confided to me several times about his concerns over her—well, her mental health. He suggested perhaps she was in the early stages of dementia or something like that."

Made sense. He'd already said as much to them. "I'll ask the detective to have the coroner look into that. Apparently an autopsy can confirm that."

The shopkeeper pressed back into her chair as though trying

to put more distance between herself and these bearers of bad news. "So undignified. Rosella didn't like hospitals or even going to the doctor. She'd be most distressed over them cutting her to bits."

Another brick toppled from Margie's heart. The two women had been friends for many years. Even suspecting Bernadette was responsible for her great-aunt's death seemed preposterous.

Still, somebody killed her.

Somebody she knew.

She laid a hand on the arm of the woman's chair. "They treat the body respectfully. And while they take samples of tissues and organs, they don't desecrate the body. Your care and concern for her is touching, however."

Bernadette jumped to her feet. "Yes, well, we were close. Not to say she was perfect. She was as changeable as the weather. As you saw by how she promised everybody and their brother an inheritance." She crossed to the front display window and stared out. "Too cruel."

Whether she meant the autopsy, the murder, her husband's death, or Aunt Rosella's treatment of her friends, Margie wasn't certain.

If the latter, they now had more suspects than they needed.

Chapter 5

After a quick lunch at a diner three doors east of the bookstore, Margie called Ted and agreed to meet at his house about ten blocks from the store.

Her grandmother commented on the tidy gardens and well-kept if older homes. "Would aspens grow in Bear Cove? I can't imagine the winters in Maine are any worse than here."

"I researched aspens for a college paper. Did you know that an aspen grove is a single living organism? All the trees there originated from one plant."

Grams turned in her seat. "I didn't."

Margie nodded as she made the last turn onto Grey Street. "It should be along here. On the right."

"What else do you know about the trees?"

"If one gets sick, most likely they all will, since they're connected through their root system. And they do better at higher altitudes. Even the ones down here in Denver don't live very long."

Her grandmother chuckled. "Down here in Denver? We're a mile above sea level. Just thinking about it gives me vertigo."

Margie extracted a bottled water from a bag behind her seat and handed it across the console. "More likely you're not drinking enough." She slowed at the address they sought. "Nope, it's true. They don't do well at sea level. Besides which, they're closely related to our east coast birch."

"True." Grandma Carly chugged half the bottle and set it in the cup holder on the dash. "I noticed something about the way they number addresses in this city."

"Oh, and what's that?"

"Well, the city follows a mostly north-south, east-west grid. The addresses on the east and the south are even numbers, while the north and west are odd." She crossed her arms over her chest. "I even made up a ditty to remember."

"And you've only been here one day. I'll bet there are long-time residents who haven't made that connection."

"Numbers are like music to me. Here goes: east is even, and south is the same."

"Cool." She picked up her purse and slung it over her shoulder. "Ready?"

"As I'll ever be. Ted Bloom isn't on my list of favorite people."

"Oh, Grams, he's just a harmless old man."

"With his eyes on the prize. Never underestimate the power of money over a person."

Margie gestured to the house, a split level on an oversized lot. "He seems to have done well for himself."

"Particularly for a handyman. Must be good money in fixing broken things."

Margie laughed. "Perhaps I should have gone into this business instead of going to college." She joined her grandmother on the sidewalk. "Think of the student loans I wouldn't have to pay back."

Grandma Carly pulled her close. "And think of all the books you wouldn't have read. All the libraries that wouldn't receive the benefit of your love for their readers and tomes. Not to mention the bookstore you are now the proud owner of."

"Would Aunt Rosella leave it to me if I'd done a different major?"

"Probably. She wanted somebody who loved her babies as much as she did. Who wouldn't sell them to just anybody. Who'd make sure they went to a good home."

Margie smiled. "Nutty as that might sound to somebody else, I totally get her." An ache filled her throat, and tears blurred her vision. "I miss her so much, and I barely knew her."

"Not your fault, dear. You had no control over when your family visited, and judging by what everybody has said about her, you had no control over when she came east." Her grandmother led the way up the walkway, lined with landscaped beds, filled with blooming plants of all colors and shapes. "She called Edgewater home."

"Did I tell you that when I talked to her last week, I said something about Denver being her home, and she corrected me. Said not Denver. Edgewater."

"Sounds like Rosella."

A quick jab to the doorbell to announce their presence, and the door opened.

"Come in, ladies. Right on time. Didn't get lost, did you?"

Grams stepped in. "No. It was easy to find since we know the streets in this area are in alphabetical order, we know where we started at 5920 West 25th Avenue, and you gave us your

54

address. Easy-peasey."

Ted blinked a couple of times, and Margie stifled a chuckle. Sometimes her grandmother could be so literal. Particularly on the subject of numbers.

"Ahem, well, yes." He gestured through the house to the sliding glass doors off the kitchen. "It's such a delightful afternoon, I thought we'd sit on the patio."

Margie followed her grandmother, and Ted locked— correction, double-locked—the door, stopping in the kitchen to extract a jug of lemonade and one of iced tea from the fridge. "Go on out. I'm right behind you."

They settled on the covered patio and the handyman offered a cold beverage. Both women chose an Arnold Palmer—half iced tea, half lemonade.

Ted poured for them. "I confess, I've never done it this way." He filled his own glass with the same and sipped. "Oh, that is nice. I rarely drink sweet tea, but this is the perfect blend." He set his glass on the table, crossed one knee over the other, and sat back. "You said you wanted to talk."

Strange way to start a conversation for out-of-town guests. No local chit-chat. Gardening tips. *How about those Rockies?*

Margie nodded. Fine, if that's how he wanted this to go. "We've been talking with the police. They are looking further into Aunt Rosella's death because certain evidence has come to light showing she didn't accidentally fall down the stairs."

He quirked his chin toward her grandmother. "I looked you up last night. Online. You've solved several murders. Your name is in the news from Maine to New Mexico. Wyoming. Arizona. You keep turning up like a bad penny."

55

Grams rose to the bait like a pro, likely developed in her years of testifying in court about folks trying to hide assets and embezzle funds. "Even a bad penny has its place when you need just one more cent."

His eyes narrowed. "So what do you want me to know?"

Her grandmother nodded to her to continue. "Tell us about Aunt Rosella."

He shrugged. "Not much to say. She owned the bookstore. Paid her bills and lived well, but whether that was due primarily to the more valuable books she often sold, I'm not sure. Perhaps. She loved books. She read all the time. We broke—" He paused, and the tips of his ears flamed. "What I mean to say is—"

Grams leaned forward. "So you argued about books?"

"Occasionally." He uncrossed then recrossed his legs in the opposite direction. "What I mean is, I felt sometimes she would rather spend an evening with a book than with me."

Not surprising. "So was your relationship on or off at the time of her death?"

He blinked again. Did he use the mannerism to give himself time to come up with an answer, or was there a lot of dust or pollen in the air?

"On again. For several months. In fact, she told me last week she was changing her will to write me in as sole beneficiary."

When her grandmother sat back, Margie took over the questioning. "So your relationship had advanced to that stage, had it?"

"What are you implying? We were good friends. Did I want more than that? Sure. Bachelor life isn't all it's cracked up to be. I'd have married her in a heartbeat, but she wouldn't hear of it.

Said she loved one man, and I wasn't him. Said she wasn't willing to give up half her income to marry again." He sighed. "It's just as well. I couldn't compete with a ghost."

"And how did that make you feel?"

"Like she was using me." He glared at the two then turned his focus back to Margie. "I fixed whatever needed fixing. Dropped everything when she called, day or night."

"Did she pay you for that work?"

"Well, yes, but that's not the point, is it? I mean, we meant something to each other."

Grams cleared her throat softly. "Is she named as a beneficiary of your will?" Her gaze took in the well-tended yard, with fountains, a pool, flower beds, a vegetable garden, a storage shed, and a larger structure, perhaps big enough for a studio or guest room. "What is sauce for the goose should be sauce for the gander, as the saying goes."

"Well, no. I mean, I rent this house. I have few assets apart from my pickup and used furniture."

Ah, a painful revelation for him, no doubt. Handyman work wasn't as lucrative as his lifestyle made it appear.

He stood. "I see what you're doing. You think I killed her. Well, I didn't."

Margie patted his chair and smiled. "Ted, you're a nice man, but you have to look at it from our perspective. We only have your word that you and Aunt Rosella were an item. That she planned to leave you—"

He returned inside the house then came back and slapped an envelope on the table. "There. You need evidence? Read that."

Margie pulled out the single folded sheet of paper and read

57

the words aloud.

My dearest Ted, thank you for a wonderful evening. I now know what I must do to make things right between us. Tomorrow I will call my attorney and have him draw up a new will naming you as my sole beneficiary. You deserve all my love and all my worldly goods. Sleep tight. Yours always, R.

She handed the note over to her grandmother then turned to Ted. "Well, it seems as though you worked yourself into her good graces again. Which makes the whole thing more puzzling than ever."

"And what's that?"

"Why didn't she do what she said?"

"Probably that weasel of a nephew got to her."

Margie shook her head. "If that was true, she'd have left the will exactly as it was, since he was already her heir." She nodded toward the letter. "Mind if we take this to compare with other samples of her handwriting?"

His brow pulled down. "Are you saying I forged this? Why would I do that?"

"Perhaps to make a claim on the estate."

He snatched the letter back and crammed it into its envelope. "No, you can't have it. You should go."

"Mind if I ask an unrelated question?"

"I might not answer."

She sighed. She'd pushed too hard and now his more obstreperous side showed. "Did Aunt Rosella ever mention hearing voices?"

"What kind of voices?"

"Not certain. Around the bookstore, perhaps."

"She always said the books talked to her."

"No, I mean real voices."

"She mentioned once that people talking outside her window one night kept her awake."

"Did she recognize the voices?"

He shook his head. "And she didn't say if it was men or women. I figured it was kids making out or hooking up or whatever they call it nowadays. She said nothing about it again."

"Thanks for your time." Margie stood and turned to her grandmother. "We have another appointment and we don't want to be late."

Grams tucked her phone into her purse and nodded, following her out the hallway. Once in the car and buckled in, Margie started the engine and turned on the air conditioner.

She leaned back in her seat. "Did we learn anything important here? I'm still keeping him on my list of suspects."

"Me, too. He seemed cagey about some aspects of their relationship. I fear he doth protest too much about the note. He was the one who suggested a forgery, when neither of us said anything about it."

Margie sighed. "I wish he'd let us take it to compare."

Her grandmother pulled her phone out of the outside pocket of her well-organized purse. "I've got the next best thing. I took a picture while you kept him occupied." She sighed. "Wish I'd thought to do that when Arthur showed us his alleged newer will. And Bernadette's so-called codicil."

"Grams, Aunt Rosella was right. Both Miss Marple and Sherlock Holmes would have been hard pressed to keep up with you." She checked the mirrors then pulled out into the street. "Now, on to see the attorney. I've got a feeling he's holding something back, too."

Grandma Carly chuckled. "And now that the hounds of the Baskervilles are on his heels, he doesn't stand a chance."

"You know the title is hound, right? One?"

"Yes, dear, but there are two of us."

Margie stopped at a four-way and laughed. "You're right. He doesn't stand a chance."

{*}

Carly watched the passing scenery through the passenger window of the car as her granddaughter navigated the quaint streets of Edgewater. Rosella's attorney lived and worked from his home off Harlan Street and West 24th Avenue, in a primarily residential area. Plenty of mature trees shaded the lots, and the pride of ownership was evident in the tidy lawns, flowers and shrubs, and even American flags on poles or hanging from eaves on many houses.

She pointed out a busy yard, enclosed by a fence, and dotted with dozens of lawn ornaments, from flamingos to Snow White and her entire ensemble. "Oh, look at that one. How cute."

Margie's nose wrinkled as though smelling week old fish. "Not for me. I like the lean and clean look."

"I wonder do they have to move that stuff to mow?"

"If it was me, I'd fix it so I didn't have any grass. They've covered almost every blade with a tacky statue of something or other."

"To each his own, I guess."

Her granddaughter pulled into a double-wide driveway devoid of any other vehicles. "Doesn't look like he has a previous client still here."

Carly checked the dash clock. "We're ten minutes early. Hopefully we can get in and out quick."

"That would be an answer to prayer, to be sure." She switched off the engine and stepped out. "Wonder what he might tell us that will help with our investigation."

"With any luck, he'll blurt out a confession, and we can conclude this. I'd like to enjoy some of my time here. Walk around Sloan's Lake. Shop downtown. Buy so many mystery books I have to get another suitcase to fly home."

"Hmm, which reminds me. I need to call the airline and see about postponing my trip back. There will be a lot of work for me here to get the store into shape."

Carly eyed the young woman over the top of the car. "Are you considering selling?"

She shrugged. "I haven't spent enough time here to decide if I want to stay. Or run for the hills." She chuckled. "Or should I say the coast? Since we're already in the hills."

"I'll go through the financials tomorrow morning and let you know how things stand. That should help with your decision."

"And while you're doing that, I'll check the inventory and see how that stands. She has a lot of books, but if they're only worth a dollar or two each, that's not much value."

"You'd have to sell a lot of books just to cover expenses. Did Rosella have a website?"

"I didn't ask. But online sales would definitely help. I'll add that to my list to check on."

"We'd best get in. I'd hate to lose our appointment to his next client."

The two arrived at the front door where a sign told them to

enter, which they did. Inside the foyer, cool and dim despite the warm temperature and bright sunlight outside, a staircase led upstairs. Against the far wall, a young woman at a desk with a computer terminal, printer, and fax machine, looked up from a document.

She tossed them a one-hundred-watt smile. "Can I help you?"

Carly stepped forward. "We have an appointment with Mr. Lowe."

The receptionist's brow pulled down, and she clicked her mouse several times. "He doesn't have a three o'clock appointment, I'm afraid. Do you have the right day?"

"Yes. He gave us the time yesterday. We're related to Rosella Hanson, and we're here to discuss her estate."

The woman paled. "Oh, that was so tragic. And she was in such good spirits last week." Her gaze moved to Margie. "Are you her great-niece?"

Margie nodded. "Yes."

"She was so excited you were coming for a visit. Said she had a big surprise for you." Her smile slipped away. "But she didn't have the chance to share it."

"No, she didn't."

A door opened, and Robert Lowe, spiffy in his suit and tie, stepped out. Apparently lawyering was every bit as formal as it had always been. Already Carly's stomach flip-flopped simply being here. As though she were back in grade school and called into the principal's office.

He nodded to her then addressed his receptionist. "Jeannie, hold my calls, please."

The young woman rose and approached. "Can I speak to you first, Mr. Lowe?"

Her lowered voice implied she preferred the conversation stay between her employer and herself, so Carly took a step back and pretended to study a lithograph of the Edgewater plat map, circa 1895, still keeping one ear tuned in. Never know what a body might learn by eavesdropping, particularly if the other parties weren't aware.

He exhaled and his eyes narrowed. "What is it?"

"Well, sir." She sidled a step closer until her nose almost touched his shoulder. Very close for an employer-employee relationship. "My paycheck bounced again this week. And I need to pay my rent and my bills."

He waved off her words but maintained their proximity. "A mistake at the bank, I'm sure. I'll check into it."

She shook her head, her brunette tresses bouncing on her shoulders. "That's what you said last week. And the week before. Now you're three weeks behind."

He towered over her, his expression dark. "That sounds like a threat."

She cringed beneath his glare then straightened her shoulders and held his gaze. "No, sir. But I need the money. And I need it this week. In a money order or certified check. Or cash."

He broke their contact by stepping back. "I don't have time for this foolishness. The bank made a mistake."

"Well, perhaps you'll have time to hire a new secretary, because if I'm not paid by Friday, I won't be back."

Jeannie returned to her desk, while the attorney spent a moment adjusting his tie.

Carly sidled another step to her left to peer more closely at the plat. She located the house which Rosella turned into a bookstore and apartment a hundred years after the creation of this drawing.

He extended his hand to her. "Good to see you." He spoke over her shoulder to the receptionist. "You and I will discuss this—uh—situation later."

Carly shook his hand. "Thank you for making time for us in your busy schedule."

He greeted her granddaughter, then gestured them into his spacious office overlooking a well-tended yard. Lace curtains allowed light in while diffusing the sunlight. Dark furniture and walls lined with law books completed the image of the quintessential attorney office.

She and Margie sat in the upholstered chairs, while Lowe settled into a high-backed leather chair behind his desk.

He opened a file from a set of stacked wooden boxes that perfectly matched his desk and beamed at them. "Well, you already know the terms of your great-aunt's will. You are her sole beneficiary."

Margie scooted forward, perching on the edge of the chair. "Arthur said he has a more recent version."

The attorney's brow lowered. "Really? He said nothing to me about that."

Carly harrumphed. "He would, if it was genuine."

Lowe scribbled a note on a pad of paper. "I'll call him and encourage him to bring the document in for me to verify." He sighed and sat back, his chair creaking. "Amazing how many worms come out of the wood in times like this."

Yes, and you're likely one of them.

She nodded. "And Ted has a note from Rosella promising to change her will in his favor." She pulled her phone from her purse and opened the camera app, scrolling to the previous image. "I took a picture, thinking perhaps you would confirm her signature."

He accepted the phone and compared the two versions. "It looks the same, but since the note predates this will, his claim won't stand up in court." He handed back the phone. "Anything else?"

Carly sighed. "You're right about worms out of the wood. Bernadette says she has a codicil naming herself as sole heir."

This time the lawyer chuckled. "This document is the final legal will."

Margie toyed with the strap on her purse, and Carly turned to her. "What's on your mind, honey?"

"I feel like I should give some of Aunt Rosella's estate to Arthur, Ted, and Bernadette. I mean, they were close to her. Closer than I was."

The attorney grunted and shook his head. "If you want to extend a small memento, that's fine. A painting, a piece of jewelry, a book of similar value, feel free. But endeavoring to include them as co-heirs will open a can of worms. It means you acknowledge their claims are valid. And they could take your gesture to court. And perhaps win, resulting in splitting the estate however many ways the court decides."

The young woman nodded. "To change the subject, did Aunt Rosella ever mention hearing voices?"

He sat back and clasped his hands behind his head. "When

65

she came in to change her will, she said somebody was conspiring to steal her babies. But she didn't know who exactly. It's why she wanted to leave everything to you. She knew you understood her passion for the books."

"So no suggestions from her who it might be?"

He shook his head. "Not to me. You might talk to Ted or Bernadette. Or Arthur."

"We did, and they didn't have any more information than you."

Grams crossed one knee over the other. "Nice set-up you have here. Working out of your house. You live upstairs?"

"I do. Like Rosella, I enjoy being close to my office. Although some days it feels like I never really leave, if you catch my drift."

"I do. I work out of my home, too. Or at least, I used to."

Margie patted her grandmother's arm. "You still do. You changed careers."

The attorney tilted his head. "Oh?"

"Sure. I used to be a forensic accountant, and now I write mysteries."

Let's see how he reacts.

"I have a strong sense of justice."

He peered at her. "I suppose you believe in good and evil."

Interesting comment from a lawyer. If not for good and evil, he'd be out of a job. "I do. Criminals should be punished, and justice should be seen to be done. Isn't that the same line of business you're in?"

"It is. Except I apply the law. And if there is any action used to bring about a conviction that is outside the law—well, let's say,

66

we all learn and do better the next time."

"Interesting outlook. Although I suppose when you defend the guilty, that's the only way to keep your conscience clear, isn't it?"

His eyes narrowed again as he studied her. "As you say."

"As executor of Rosella's estate, how much will you receive in compensation?"

"Well, that is a private matter—"

Margie shook her head. "Actually, it isn't. It's right there in the will." She pointed to the document. "A very generous three percent." She turned to Carly. "Two percent is the norm."

The lawyer's neck flushed. "Yes, well, the estate isn't huge. And it will take extra time to settle because of—"

Now the truth was coming out. "Because of the multiple contenders for chief beneficiary, you mean?" She folded her arms over her chest. "If you recognized there could be problems, why not encourage her to mention the other three in the will? Leave them something?"

"No, that's not what I was going to say. I meant, because the sole beneficiary lived out of state, probate could take longer. Be more complicated."

"Except Margie may choose to live here. Isn't that really what Rosella wanted?"

"Well, yes, of course she hoped her niece would take over the business and keep the store going. But if not—"

"Rosella was a skinflint. She wouldn't have dreamt of paying you or anybody else a higher fee than required by law. And she wouldn't leave the store to Margie unless she believed the business would continue." She settled back and drew a couple of

67

breaths. "How much is the estate worth? Ballpark."

He exhaled sharply. "If the inventory she gave me proves out, along with the value of the property, I would say in the neighborhood of a million dollars."

"Giving you a quick and tidy profit of some thirty thousand dollars." She stood. "Time to let Mr. Lowe get on with his business." When she reached the door, she turned. "Tell Jeannie not to quit just yet. Looks like you'll be able to meet payroll."

Chapter 6

Thursday morning, after a quick breakfast of coffee and sweet rolls from the bakery across the street, Margie headed down to the bookstore to go through inventory, while her grandmother spread the financial records on the kitchen table.

When she unlocked the door from the hallway to the store, she flicked on the lights and paused in the doorway, inhaling the unique scents of paper, dust, and old wood. In a flash, she was seven years old again, spending a rainy Saturday afternoon in her local library in Riverdale, Maine.

Thankfully, today she had no concerns about Arthur getting under her feet or her skin—a quick call to him the evening before told him to take the day off. And while at first he flubbered and complained, she finally caved in and promised to pay him for the short notice. At least he'd processed those books.

For a man with so many important business meetings on his schedule, he depended on the meager earnings from the store.

Or perhaps he made more off his aunt than she realized.

If so, Grandma Carly would uncover his thieving.

And if he'd hidden his trail, perhaps the inventory check would cast a light on the dark recesses of his weaselly heart.

She glanced at the several hundred pages of books by title in

70

her hand, printed from Aunt Rosella's computer last night. Had she bitten off more than she could chew? Perhaps she should have enlisted Arthur's help.

She shook her head. She could do this. She was a capable woman. Strong-willed. Determined. Physically healthy. How difficult could it be, after all?

After printing the list the previous evening, she'd perused the items and deciding on a plan of action. While most of the books were valued at less than five dollars each, that category comprised less than twenty-five percent of the value of the books on the list.

The remaining seventy-five percent of the value came from books of greater value, with about ten percent invested in first editions and collector's items, highly prized by her great-aunt for their historical value and contribution to the genre.

She'd start there. If anybody was stealing, those would be the books they'd seek.

She set the papers on the counter by the cash register and uncapped the yellow highlighter from the drawer. Beneath the glass surface, several books rested, cushioned in black velvet. She flipped to the latter part of the list and let her finger do the walking.

The Shadow Over Innsmouth. First edition. Dust Jacket. 1936.

A little outside her great-aunt's norm of straight mystery, the slightly edgy horror was still a pride and joy for her. And valued at over five thousand dollars, the most expensive book in her collection.

Yep, there it sat, nestled in velvet, front and center. Alongside a handwritten card that read GLOVES ONLY!! $5,295.00.

She highlighted that one and moved to the next. *The Talented*

Mr. Ripley. First edition, 1955. Check.

The Dain Curse. Her aunt couldn't resist owning a few Dashiell Hammetts. First edition, 1929. Hardcover. A thousand dollars.

And the next. *The Thin Man.* Not a first—did any of those even exist outside museums? But the autograph made this one worth more than most firsts—but wait. It wasn't in the case.

Where might Aunt Rosella have put it? Nothing in the notes column to show special treatment. If she pushed the other books a little tighter together, there was room for the book.

To prove her point, she did just that, and revealed a faded section of cloth that suggested a different set up of the books in the past. Along with a price card, again with the glove admonition.

She turned and studied the shelving behind the counter where Arthur showed her other higher-priced books. Not there in alphabetical by title or by author, although, honestly, she couldn't really discern—oh, wait. By year of publication. Still not there, in its place between *The Nine Tailors* by Dorothy L. Sayers, published in 1934 and *The Maltese Falcon* of 1930.

She checked both off her list. Should she stop and look for the missing book, or continue down the list? Determined to accomplish at least one task, she chased down the rest of the books. Perhaps the inventory hadn't updated with the sale of *The Thin Man.* But, there should be a record of a check or credit card sale, in which case she'd confirm that with Grams.

But first, the list.

Three hours later, exhausted and covered with dust, Margie perched on the stool once again and scanned the list. Besides the first book identified as missing, she'd found two others. *Monkshood* of the Brother Cadfael series, one of her personal favorites because of its history and personalities, along with a little-known title by Raymond Chandler, *The Little Sister*. At four hundred dollars and one hundred, neither particularly valuable.

Which meant somebody could steal books from her great-aunt, testing out their system by starting with books they hoped she wouldn't miss.

But to blatantly remove one from the display case—well, that was bold.

Unless that theft occurred after Aunt Rosella's death.

Or its removal precipitated the murder.

Time to check the apartment and perhaps enlist Grandma Carly's help.

Surely there was a logical explanation, such as a delay in bookkeeping entries. Or the fuzzy mind of an old lady.

Because otherwise, as her pastor used to say, "If a man lies to you, he'll steal from you. And if he steals from you, he'll kill you."

She was certain that didn't apply only to the male gender, either.

{*}

Carly shrugged kinks out of her shoulders at the footsteps coming up the stairs. A glance at the clock revealed she'd invested more than three hours poring over Rosella's financial records, and she'd found several entries she was certain Margie would find interesting.

"Is that you, Margie?"

"Yep." Her granddaughter emerged through the doorway,

73

looking a little frazzled around the edges as she headed for the kitchen. "Time for a break?"

"I should say so. The coffee and sweet rolls were delish, but I'm hungry. What do we have on hand?"

Margie peered into the refrigerator. "I thought I'd make egg salad sandwiches."

"Perfect." She pulled open several cabinets until she located a saucepan. "I'll start the water. Do we have bread?"

"We do. And mayo. And even a tomato that would probably survive an atomic bomb."

Carly chuckled as she ran water into the pot and set it on the gas stovetop. "Nothing is as good as one fresh from the garden." She turned and leaned against the counter. "How was your search?"

"Discovered some interesting books missing. While the eggs are cooking, I'll look around the apartment. It's possible she brought them up here to read and then didn't want to let them go."

"Did she have an area where she prepared shipments or packages?"

"Oh, I hadn't thought about that."

"I'll check the hallway going to the parking lot. There were several doors which must lead somewhere."

"Great." Margie pulled her cell phone from her pocket and tapped the screen several times. "Setting a timer for the eggs so we don't forget them."

"Good idea. I'll check downstairs. You look wrung out. Why don't you wash your face and sit for a bit?"

Margie agreed and headed for the bathroom, and Carly went

74

down past the bookstore entrance to the hallway. The first door she came to held a furnace, now quiet; a water heater; the central air mechanism; and a stack of folded cardboard boxes.

The next door led into a laundry room, complete with ironing board and iron, all tidy and ready for use.

Across the hallway, a third door revealed a washroom for staff and customers. She made a mental note to empty the trash and replenish the soap and paper towels. And an extra roll of toilet tissue.

Behind the fourth and final door was the area she sought: a work table, complete with packing materials and a large roll of brown wrapping paper. At the end of the large worktable, a tablet with a keyboard and mouse indicated that either Rosella or Arthur was more computer-savvy than she gave them credit for.

She powered up the tablet. No password. She made another mental note to remind Margie to secure the system.

On a table along the wall, cans of glue stacked beside a set of knives that a surgeon would envy rested beside several projects under repair. Seemed Rosella did some bookbinding also.

She glanced around the room. Perhaps outgoing parcels awaited shipping or pickup.

Nope, nothing here.

Dust and something else—glue?—tickled her nose as she headed toward the stairs, when a voice caught her attention.

A man's voice.

Then a woman's. Giggling. High-pitched. Flirtatious.

She tipped her head to listen. Coming from the air ducts.

Certain they weren't anywhere on this floor since she'd just completed searching the rooms, she trotted to the bottom of the steps. "Margie. Come quick. And be quiet."

A chair scraped on the wooden floor above, then the pitter-patter of her granddaughter's footsteps overhead toward her.

Margie's pale face appeared at the railing. "What is it?" Her hoarse whisper communicated her concern in volumes. "What's happening?"

"Shh, come down. Quietly."

When Margie joined her, Carly led the way to the packing room. "Listen."

The voices continued on and off, interspersed with long moments of silence. Or near silence. The occasional groan—no, moan—and Carly's cheeks heated.

Somebody was—making out—within earshot.

She frowned. "Maybe this is how Rosella heard the voices. Through the air ducts."

"There's nobody upstairs."

"And I checked down here. So they must be near an intake or outlet vent outside." She gripped her granddaughter's hand. "Do you want to come with, or would you rather wait in here?"

Margie's face broke into a smile wide enough to split her face. "Are you kidding me? This is the most fun I've had since I got here. Apart from setting that snooty attorney head over keester."

"Okay. But I'll lead the way. And if there's any trouble, call the cops, okay?"

"Cross my heart and hope to—well, you know what I mean."

A shiver ran up and down Carly's back as the two crept to the parking lot door, which she eased open. She peeked around the barrier. Nobody in the lot. She gestured for Margie to follow her, although she suspected a herd of elephants couldn't have restrained the woman at this point.

Bending at the waist and hoping nobody saw them, she tip-toed toward the rear of the house, slowing as she neared the corner.

A quick glance and she snapped back out of sight, knocking her head against her granddaughter's arm. "There's somebody back there. Two somebodies."

"Do you recognize them?"

She giggled. "I do. Arthur. And Ginger."

"What are they doing?"

"Canoodling."

Margie's eyes widened then she laughed. "That's not a word I expected to hear used in the same sentence with Arthur's name."

"I agree. But it gets me thinking."

"About what?"

"Rosella wasn't hearing things. Perhaps somebody was meeting out here to contrive a plan to steal from her. To make her sound crazy. Maybe they hoped to get her committed and take over her business."

"It wasn't about the bookstore specifically. There's a lot of money tied up in rare books in her inventory. And some are missing. Had she figured out what they were doing? Confronted them?"

"I like the way your mind works."

Margie wrapped her arms around herself. "Except I'm worried it got her killed."

Over lunch, Margie broached the subject of their independent searches: theft of one sort or another. "So who could get that close to her to steal from her?"

"Just about any of the four people we've already talked to. Arthur worked with her, and he has a key to the house, so he could come and go when she wasn't here."

Margie nodded. "It would be easy enough for him to steal rare books. She did the research and identified the ones most valuable. Even set them up in the display case or on the shelves behind the register. Besides the books I couldn't locate—which might be explained away as a forgetful old lady putting them in a biscuit can—I found evidence that the books in the case were rearranged to disguise the fact at least one treasure is missing."

"And I found notations in her cash journal indicating she had the same suspicions."

"Her what?"

Grams chuckled as she nibbled the end of her sandwich. She washed down the bite with a gulp of water. "The more water I drink, the more clear-headed I feel. And fewer aches, too." She drained her glass. "Cash journal. She was old school. She kept her daily sales in a journal, then transferred that to the accounting system. Cash sales, checks, credit cards, online sales."

"So she had a website?"

A quick nod. "Seems so. I didn't check it out, so you'll likely want to update it. Add inventory. Offer something like a blog, ideas on how to properly store old books. Identifying valuable books. Rebinding. Like that."

"Doesn't that kind of defeat the purpose, though? I mean, I

want people to come in, buy on the spur of the moment. Bring their old books to me and let me spend the time finding a buyer and making the lion's share of the profits. Not doing that for themselves." Margie paused and toyed with her sandwich. "Wait a minute. That sounds very selfish, doesn't it?"

"Now you're getting it. Running a business is about developing a relationship. If they think you're only in it for how many books you can foist on them, they won't come here. They can do that online and not have to explain why they aren't buying every book you recommend."

"Right. I want them to come in, feel like I only want them to walk out with exactly what they want. Even if they don't know it yet themselves." She thought a moment. "Kinda like when I talk to people about my faith. I don't want to make it all about me. Instead, I want to tell them what Jesus did for me."

"Exactly. And in business, as in faith, if you offer them something they perceive has value, for no cost, then they'll keep coming back. Particularly if you also provide an expanded version of that service, even for a price."

"I get it. So many people I talk to think that loving Jesus is all about what they have to give up. The cost. And I point them back to the price paid for them already." Margie sighed. "Two first-year business courses and some Sunday school classes doesn't cover the personal aspect of either business or faith."

"It's something I learned, the hard way, over the years." A half-smile tickled her grandmother's lips. "I watched you and your parents for a long time before I finally admitted I wanted what you had."

Margie nodded. "Mom told me. I didn't understand what

took you so long."

"I'd heard the lies, too, about all the things I wouldn't be able to do anymore. But as I thought about it, most I didn't want. The closer I came to making a choice, the more clear it all became." Grams pushed her now-empty plate aside. "Who else is high on our suspect list?"

"Ted. He wanted to marry Aunt Rosella, but she told him she didn't want to lose half her pension. She was a shrewd old lady."

Her grandmother laughed. "That's what we should put on her headstone."

"And mine."

"Me, too. And let's not forget Bernadette. She could disguise herself. And she had that codicil."

"And the attorney needed the money the probate would provide."

Grams' eyes narrowed. A sure sign she was thinking. "Wonder why? Seems like apart from paying the secretary, his overhead is low."

"Perhaps there's a leaking valve on the other end of the income pipeline."

"Interesting way to look at it. A visit back to Jeannie would be helpful."

"And while we're talking to people again, let's find out who had the means. After all, long-lasting insulin isn't something you can buy over the counter." She stood and cleared the table. "I'll chat up Jeannie and Bernadette. They might be more likely to talk to me alone. And you can take on the men."

Her grandmother groaned then brightened. "I'll pretend to

be Miss Marple. People always talk to dithery old women."

Margie patted her arm. "Then they'll be sorely mistaken. You are anything but."

"I'll lure them into a false sense of security."

{*}

Two hours later, Carly arrived back at the house, dropped off by an online fleet taxi, just as Margie pulled into the parking lot. Perfect timing.

She paid the driver and waited at the door while her granddaughter pulled two grocery bags from the backseat and headed her way.

Margie held up a bag. "Thought we might like a proper dinner. To keep our brains nourished. Steak. Shrimp. Salad. How does that sound?"

"Like I died and went to heaven." She snagged a bag to free a hand for her granddaughter to unlock the door. "Were your forays successful?"

"Yes. And yours?"

"Very. But let's get inside before—" She glanced around. "Before those steaks warm up too much."

'But Grandma—"

Carly ushered the younger woman into the house and close the door behind them. "I want you to run upstairs to the kitchen and talk at a normal tone of voice. I'm going out to that vent and see if I can hear you. We don't want to alert the enemy as to what we're up to."

Her granddaughter's eyes turned into moons with a blue center, but she did as she was told. In the meantime, Carly skulked around the rear of the house and situated herself in the same place Arthur and Ginger previously occupied.

As she waited, she surveyed the alleyway. Not wide enough for a trash truck or other automobile traffic, the spot held wheeled trash cans and a recycling bin. Further down, behind another house, a barbeque grill and pop-up canopy suggested a more domestic use of the space.

After about five minutes, she returned to the house and called to her granddaughter from the base of the stairs. "Did you talk?"

Margie peered around the doorjamb. "I talked. I shouted. I screamed. I sang. You didn't hear me?"

"No." Which meant only one thing. The exhaust fan over the store is too high up. "I heard the voices before when I was in the work room. There must be an exhaust vent to the outside because of the glue. There has to be some other way up here where the sound would travel."

Margie snapped her fingers. "The window in the spare room where we're sleeping. I tried to open it this morning because I wanted some of the cooler air in. But it's painted in place. Open about a half an inch."

Carly hurried to the room and peered down. Overlooking the alley and the next yard over the fence, the view was nothing to write home about.

But if somebody was holding a conversation down there, a person with good hearing might just be able to discern their presence, if not their actual words.

She turned to her granddaughter. "So now we know Rosella wasn't losing her mind, no matter what Arthur says. She really heard people talking."

"And I learned something else that might be important."

Carly smiled. "I always think better when I'm making dinner. Let's head that way."

Once they found a frying pan for onions, she volunteered to chop while Margie scrubbed potatoes for the microwave. "Were Jeannie and Bernadette open to talk with you?"

"Yes. Jeannie said her boss was okay to work for, but she didn't trust him since he's cheating on his wife. Apparently his mistress just had a baby, a son, and now she's pressing him for money for support and expenses."

"Running one household costs a lot, let alone two."

Her granddaughter set the spuds on the turntable and pressed the button to cook. "Ten minutes. Ready to sear the steaks?"

"Ready." Carly set the meat on the grill pan and slid it into the preheated oven to broil. "Any idea where he might get insulin?"

"His mistress is a nurse." Her granddaughter found another pan and added hot water from the sink before dropping a bag of frozen e-z peel shrimp in. "About six minutes for them. We can peel 'em as we eat."

"Yummy. Did you remember—"

"Cocktail sauce? Of course. And horseradish. Couldn't remember if Aunt Rosella had any in her fridge." She pulled butter from the fridge and set it on the table. "For the potatoes." She followed up by dumping a salad kit into a large bowl. "Gotta love the convenience.'

"So probably no trouble with means if he asked her nicely." She grinned. "You are a brilliant investigator. How about

83

Bernadette?"

"Well, she tried the codicil on me again, suggesting perhaps we could come to an agreement so she wouldn't contest the will. Not in those words exactly, of course, but we both understood what she meant. I didn't jump on that, but I asked her if she had a favorite painting or piece of furniture in mind that Aunt Rosella might have given her. She mentioned an emerald brooch that perfectly matched her eyes."

"Then Bernadette must be color blind, along with her other problems, since her eyes are grey, not green. What about her means?"

"Her husband was a diabetic, and when the longer-lasting insulin came on the market, it was such a blessing to him. He struggled to maintain his blood sugar before, but did much better afterwards."

"Did she mention the brooch again?"

"She did. I put her off, telling her I had to wait until we valued the estate."

"Unless she turns out to be the killer, of course."

"There is that." Margie quirked her chin toward the oven. "Time to check the steaks."

Carly gave another quick stir to the onions then wiped her hands. "On it." She flipped the meat and set the pan back. "Three more minutes should do it."

Margie carried silverware and glasses to the table, then set their plates on the stovetop to warm. "How about you? You said you learned some stuff, too."

"Well, let's see." She checked off her results on her fingers. "Arthur is a weasel, and a diabetic to boot. When I pressed him on what kind of insulin he used, he bawked. I said I had a friend who was a diabetic, and she wears a pump, and did he use one."

"Did he buy it?"

Margie blinked several times. "What makes you think I wasn't telling the truth?"

"That little tic near your left eye. Gives you away now just as it did when you were little."

"Okay, I 'fess up. No friend who is a diabetic." Her granddaughter filled their water glasses and added ice. "He said he prefers to control his insulin himself and uses a combination of long- and short-term."

"So he had the means." Carly turned off the broiled and extracted the steaks. "Oh, these look perfect. Want to cut yours to check it?"

"Nope. I trust your grill skills." Margie set her choice on a plate. "Potatoes are here. Toppings are on the table."

"Great." Carly filled her plate and headed to the dining room. "Want to say grace?"

"Sure."

They bowed their heads and held hands, and Carly's heart swelled as her granddaughter lifted their thanks and praises for their meal, their safekeeping, and their investigatory endeavors to the throne of grace.

She sighed and opened her eyes after the amen. "That was beautiful. And heartfelt. The food will taste better for sure."

"Before you fill your mouth with steak, what else did you learn? Although I'm kind of hoping you don't have more names to add to the list. Three is already enough, don't you think?"

"I do, but unfortunately, there are four. Turns out Ted's

sister is a pharmacist. So, just like Robert Lowe, he has access to insulin, if he can convince his sister to supply it for him."

"Which would be highly illegal and unethical, wouldn't it?"

"Yes." Carly cut off a forkful of steak and popped it into her mouth before her granddaughter complained. "Oh, that is good. You chose well, child."

"So we have Arthur and Bernadette on the top of the list. With Ted and Lowe close behind."

"Looks like it. Now, let's enjoy our dinner before it gets cold, then we can talk more."

"Sounds like a plan."

{*}

After dinner, Margie led the way into the living room. Their tummies full, a long day of hard work behind them, and what did they have to show for all their effort? Two suspects tied for first place, and two more locked in second.

Now she knew how the jury in *Twelve Angry Men* felt. Deadlocked.

She propped her feet on the coffee table across from her grandmother and leaned her head back. "Where do we go now?"

"I don't know." Grams sipped her decaf java and set the cup on the side table at her elbow. "Seems like we've got the how, most likely the why, but the who evades us."

Margie nodded and picked up the cloisonné clock Aunt Rosella insisted she bring with her. "Wonder why it was so important I drag this with me?"

Grams shrugged. "Beats me. Why don't you wind it up? Maybe it chimes on the hour. Or sings a song."

She wound up the mechanism with the small ring key on the

back and set it on the table. "Hmm. Doesn't seem to work." She tapped the case. "Still nothing." She sighed. "Any ideas?"

"Did Rosella put in packing material to protect the insides?"

Margie smacked her forehead. "Duh." She checked the back of the case then picked up her steak knife. "It's got three tiny screws holding the back in place." She undid the back and set it and its fasteners on the table. "There's paper in here." She maneuvered the material out then unfolded it. "Wowzers. It's a code."

Her grandmother scooted over to sit on the loveseat beside her. "Ooh, I love codes."

"Good. Because I don't have a clue what it means. And Aunt Rosella didn't tell us anything or leave a note on this, either."

Grams read out the contents. "4R. 6D. 1L. 2U. 12." She turned the piece over. "Nothing on the back. Wonder what it means?"

"No idea. A safe combination?"

"A hiding place?"

"Knowing Aunt Rosella, that makes more sense."

Her grandmother chuckled. "I've seen movies and books where numbers and letters like this were about bricks in a fireplace. But she doesn't have one."

"Or flagstones on a patio. Ditto."

"Then it has to be about books. Her passion. It's just like Rosella to use a book to hide something important. Without this code, the chances of somebody finding the specific book must be slim, so it's not likely one of the everyday mysteries on the regular sale shelves."

Margie snapped her fingers. "The shelves behind the

register."

The two women stared at each other a moment, then Margie jumped to her feet, the slip of paper in her hand. "Coming?"

Her grandmother beat her to the top of the stairs, and the two stampeded to the bookstore like a couple of kids. Margie grinned. If nothing else, this mystery injected new life and new purpose into her grandmother.

And herself, too, truth be told.

Behind the counter, they stared at the floor-to-ceiling shelving of higher-priced books.

Margie checked the first clue. "Okay. 4R. Four right?"

"Four books? No, more likely four sections." She counted off the number. "Next?"

"6D."

"Six down." Grams numbered the shelves. "That brings us to here." She laid a finger on a shelf at her eye level. "The next one?"

"One left, I presume."

They worked through the remaining clue, arriving at a shelf at her grandmother's eye level. "Now, twelve. No direction. Must mean the twelfth book." She counted across, left to right. "Of course. *A Study in Scarlet.*"

"But now what? That's the last clue."

"Then twelve must be the same direction. Page twelve." Grandma Carly flipped to the page and scanned the words. "Aunt Rosella was a sharp cookie. This part of the story is about poisons and a prick on the finger."

"So we have our suspects. We have proof that Aunt Rosella was trying to leave a clue in case of her death. Now what?"

"Now I need to sleep on all this. Sometimes the answer comes when I rest from trying to figure it out."

"Do you have any ideas?"

Her grandmother smiled. "Just unsubstantiated suspicions of a dithery old lady that I'm certain will come together when I least expect."

Margie didn't want to wait. Didn't want to sleep on it. But as Grams headed for the stairs and then their room, it appeared she didn't have much choice.

Just as in her faith life, being patient was just as important in an investigation.

Did she have what it took?

Grams thought so.

And so did Aunt Rosella.

Chapter 7

Carly awoke with a start the following morning. Friday. If she was to have any time to relax over the weekend, she must solve this mystery today. Preferably this morning.

A quick trip to the bathroom, then she dressed before heading to the kitchen for coffee. Margie beat her to it. Coffee bubbled in the old-fashioned electric percolator, and the delicious scent of cinnamon buns wafted from the direction of the oven.

Carly planted a kiss on her favorite granddaughter's cheek. "You are so special."

"Couldn't sleep. Got up and showered. Did you come up with anything?"

"I think so. But let's eat first."

Margie shook her head. "Not a chance. I need answers. Now."

"Okay. Don't let those cinnamon buns burn, and I'll go down and get the clue."

A quick high five. "Deal."

Carly skipped down the stairs and into the bookstore, snagged *A Study in Scarlet* from its place on the shelf, then trotted upstairs. Margie pulled the pan of rolls from the oven, and they each served themselves a double portion and a large mug of coffee, then headed for the dining room.

Carly set the old book on the table. "I'll say grace this morning." She did so, quickly and efficiently if less eloquently than her granddaughter had the previous evening, then shook her head while buttering her roll. "Not until I get sustenance and caffeine into my system."

Margie sputtered her resistance. Ah, the sense of control was exhilarating.

Still, she wouldn't torture the girl for long. "I thought about the book a lot last night. Hard to believe Rosella would have gone to all that trouble for the simple clue of finding the book. All that did was confirm what we believed all along. That she thought somebody was out to harm her."

"You mean she hid another clue in the book?" Margie swiped at a drizzle of frosting on her chin. "How did we miss it?"

"We were too busy celebrating our discovery of the book and the clue." Carly sipped her coffee, enjoying the heat to the tip of her toes. Despite the promise of temperatures in the high eighties later in the day, the high altitude evenings were cool. "So let's take a look. First, page twelve."

She flipped to the page and studied the words, then held the book to the light coming in through the large double window. "No evidence of invisible ink. No characters off kilter. Nothing—wait a minute. What's that?" She picked at the top outside corner of the page. "It's like there are two pages stuck—there are. Pass me a clean knife."

"You aren't planning to mar a valuable book by cutting apart pages missed in the binding process, are you?"

She paused, the knife poised near the edge. "Not being able

to read it makes it more valuable?"

"It might. Depends on what a collector is looking for."

"How much is this one worth?"

"Over two thousand dollars."

"Do you want to solve this mystery or not?"

Margie sighed. "Go ahead. Vandalize a national treasure."

"Well, it's not like it's in the Smithsonian or something."

She tucked the tip of the knife into the small opening where the two pages came unstuck then eased the pages apart. A quarter-folded piece of paper dropped into her lap.

"Well, well, what do we have here?" She set the book aside and unfolded the sheet. "An inventory of Rosella's most valuable books, and their locations in the store." She slid the sheet across to Margie. "Did you find everything on that list?"

Margie scanned the paper. "No. I didn't find any of these. They weren't on the inventory. Which means the estate is worth a lot more than we first estimated. Plus, the three books I couldn't find aren't on this one, which means they came in after she wrote this note but before she died." She checked the date at the top. "And Aunt Rosella made this list less than two weeks ago. Just before she mailed my clock."

"Makes sense. She'd need the note to put in the clock. And she likely wouldn't make up the clue and leave the book to chance, in case she sold it."

"I just had a thought. Hold on." Margie sifted through her papers until she came up with the inventory list. "That's what I remembered."

"Are you going to share?"

"*A Study in Scarlet* isn't on the inventory. She must have left it off so it didn't get sold accidentally."

"Or if anybody checked the computer, they wouldn't find the book and try to steal it."

Margie stared at the list in her hand. "You know what this means, don't you?"

"Time to enlist the help of the police. And to assemble the suspects."

"All of them?"

"All four. I want to see them squirm." Carly rubbed her hands together. "Oh, this is my favorite part."

Her granddaughter chuckled. "You really are like Miss Marple, aren't you? That's what she always does."

"Well, so does Hercule Poirot, and nobody would dare call him dithery."

"And nobody better call you that either when I'm around, or they'll have to answer to me."

{*}

Margie disconnected her cell phone. "Detective Hogan wasn't happy. He said he felt like a Keystone cop in a bad comedy. But after I shared our information and what we suspected, he agreed to call the Gang of Four and assemble them in the bookstore in an hour."

"Great. That gives us just time to create a comfy conversation pit and brew a new pot of coffee. No food, though. Too much fuss."

She chuckled. "Grandma, you sound like you're in your element."

"I am. This is the best part of the mystery."

"So you know who did it?"

"I do. And why."

"Going to share with me?"

"Nope. Just follow my lead, and it will all become apparent as we go along." Her grandmother finished the last of her roll and washed it down with the final swig of coffee. "Okay. Let's go."

Ten minutes before the hour expired, Margie pushed the last chair into place, creating a cozy but perhaps not so comfortable circle of chairs, seven in total. Including the detective in the seating plan seemed the civil thing to do. Additional officers would wait in the hallway. Out of sight. And at the rear of the building and around the corner in case their chief suspect tried to make a run for it.

She chuckled at the running commentary her greying grandmother offered to defend her choices in where each should sit, why she wanted to offer coffee but not tea, and the order of service, as she called it. How she'd explain what they knew, tying all the clues and information into a tidy package.

At five 'til, the detective entered the store. "I've positioned officers around the building out of sight." He glanced at the chairs. "Where do you want me to sit?"

Margie shook her head. "Don't ask me. This is her party."

"I'd like you there with your back to the inside door, if that works for you." Grams gestured to the overstuffed high-backed chair. "Nobody will come in that way, so you won't mind having your back to that door."

He grinned. "You know us LEO's too well."

They'd lost her. "LEO's?"

Her grandmother laid a hand on her arm. "Police speak for law enforcement officers. They don't sit where they can't see who's coming in."

He nodded. "Legend is it goes back to the killing of Doc Halliday, shot by a man coming in from behind him."

"Gotcha." She arched an eyebrow. "A lot to learn."

The door opened, and Arthur and Bernadette entered, glaring at each other as they jostled for position in the door opening.

Carly, a painful introvert, acted as though she hosted murder mystery parties every day. Margie marveled at the way she greeted these two like treasured guests, asking how they were and how they liked their coffee.

But before she filled their orders, Ted and the attorney entered, pointedly ignoring each other as though they were on different planets. Which they probably were. In their minds, at least.

Margie delivered coffee to their first three attendees while Carly turned her charm on the final two.

After each greeted—or didn't—the others, Grandma Carly cleared her throat and waited until all eyes focused on her. "Thanks for coming. I'm sure it wasn't how you envisioned spending an hour or so this morning. But let me assure you, your attendance is crucial so we can solve the mystery of why Rosella died."

Arthur snorted. "She fell down the stairs."

Ted shook his head. "After somebody jabbed her with insulin. It was murder."

Rosella's nephew glared at him. "You got a double indemnity policy on her or something? It was an accident."

Detective Hogan shifted in his chair, and the Gang of Four

quieted again. "I understand this is unorthodox, but please, let Mrs. Turnquist continue."

Grams dug into her pants pocket then checked the other one before pulling out a slip of paper. Margie saw through that ploy: let them think she was dumber than a brick. A traditional Columbo trick.

She held up the note. "This is a clue Rosella sent to Margie in a clock. We thought the clock was a clue, but we were wrong."

Arthur snorted. Again. "Why doesn't that surprise me?"

Carly fixed a steely gaze on him. "No comments from the peanut gallery unless I ask you a direct question. Understood, son?"

He glared at her, mouth working as though to respond, then his shoulders slumped, and he nodded. "Yes, ma'am."

"Good." Carly unfolded the note. "Here we have a series of numbers and letters, which we followed to this." She held up *A Study in Scarlet*. "The final clue referred to the number of the book on the shelf and the page she wanted us to see." She opened the book. "On page twelve, we see references to poisons and a finger prick. She anticipated her death, by a poisonous substance, by needle or some other form of injection."

Bernadette leaned forward. "Insulin isn't a poison."

Detective Hogan crossed one knee over the other. "To a non-diabetic, it is."

Her Grams continued. "She reported to several of you she heard voices. People conspiring to harm her. Well, we figured out how that happened. What she heard was voices coming from outside, either through an exhaust duct or through a partially opened window." She fastened her gaze on Arthur. "Sometimes

97

the source was innocent. A couple cuddling."

Her weaselly cousin at least had the good grace to blush, but he remained silent as instructed. Maybe he *was* redeemable.

Instantly, Margie's heart moved a notch closer to tender for her cousin. Everybody was salvageable, weren't they? After all, was her sin any less than his? And look at how much she'd changed once she finally understood God's love for her. She and Arthur should have a chat soon.

Ted grunted. "And the other times?"

Grams shrugged. "Children playing in the alley. A homeless person. The house down the street has a grill, so maybe they had a party." Her eyes roved the group, but this time she didn't light on any particular person. "Or perhaps the murderer met with an accomplice. Or somebody who had no idea what they were up to." She paused and tapped the book again. "Last night I recognized the importance of this book in yet another way, confirming this was the book she meant us to find."

The four suspects broke out into a babble of complaints and questions until Margie couldn't stand it any longer. She stood and clapped her hands twice. "If you'd wait, you'll hear answers to your questions, and the innocent will leave."

After resuming her seat, her grandmother continued. "*The Adventure of the Abbey Grange* was the first usage of a now-famous Sherlock Holmes quote."

Arthur's brow pulled down. "And what does that have to do with why we're here?"

Grams glared at him. "The murder in that story was first thought to be a robbery. Which Holmes later proved incorrect." She sat forward. "Rosella knew the person who would ultimately

98

kill her so well that she even figured out *how* they'd do it."

Bernadette tapped a toe on the floor, beating out a tune without a melody. "This isn't one of your little mystery stories, Carly. This is real life."

"True. Very real. And it's also not a television show where the actors will appear next week in another program. Rosella is very dead. And will remain so." She set the book aside. "When Rosella called Margie to ask for help, she said something which sounded strange. *The game is afoot.*"

Arthur snorted, hesitated, then raised his hand. "May I ask a question?"

Grams nodded. "Go ahead."

"I always wondered what that meant."

Her grandmother smiled, a Mona Lisa-like smile, as though she possessed all the answers to all the secrets in the world. "It means that we must now hunt down our quarry. Rosella knew her Holmes."

Robert Lowe, who had been quiet up to this point, leaned forward, elbows on his knees. "I suppose you'll go through the reasons each of us is here."

"Correct. I'll lay out your motive, your opportunity, and your means. In court, a prosecutor must prove each element beyond a reasonable doubt to gain a conviction. For the innocent, at least one of those elements will be missing or will be cloudy. Bear with me."

Margie sat back in her chair and studied each of the suspects as her grandmother ran through the list they'd already discussed. When she ended, each of the four were still on the hook.

Grams stood, her back to the counter, framed by Aunt

Rosella's most valuable books. Margie envisioned her on the cover of *Writers Digest* in the near future, as feature author for the month.

"Each of you had all three elements. But then Rosella's clues led us to the deciding factor. The list of her most valuable books and where she hid them. One interesting thing was that none of the books Margie identified when she completed an inventory is on that list. And another is that a quick check of the store reveals that all of the books are in their appointed places." She turned to face Arthur. "So the books you were taking weren't her most valuable, although the money you received for selling them might have made it seem so. Besides, you're too tall." Then she turned to Ted. "And your disappointment with her when she broke her promise to change her will to favor you wasn't enough to propel you to kill her."

He smirked up at her. "And how are you so certain?"

"A quick call to your sister let you off the hook. I'm uncertain whether she was more upset with my suggestion she might provide you with an illegal drug, or with the allegation that you asked. You're also taller than her early-morning visitor."

"Thank you. I loved Rosella."

"And I believe you. But you were willing to contest her last wishes with that love letter."

"It was just a bluff to see how you'd react."

"Uh-huh." She faced the attorney. "As for you, I don't understand why Rosella didn't see through your façade and fire you long ago."

The attorney's eyes stayed glued to the floor. "She was in love with my father once. A long time ago. She would have married him. But then my father made the mistake of getting mixed up with my mother, and one thing led to another. I was born five months after their shotgun wedding."

"Makes sense. Rosella always had a sentimental streak. But as with Ted and Arthur—"

Bernadette stood. "I can see where this is leading. Let the men off so that means I killed her. Well, you're wrong. I loved her."

Grams nodded. "You're right. In the past tense, unfortunately. You, too, were stealing from Rosella. Small things. Cash from the drawer which she initially blamed on Arthur. She shrugged off his shortcomings, believing men need their little indulgences. After all, he was family. But then it happened when Arthur called in sick, so it wasn't him. Didn't take her long to figure out who. She made notes in her cash journal. She was so disappointed."

The wig lady pointed a finger toward her. "She was always so trusting. Leaving the cash register unlocked and going to the bathroom. I'd come over for coffee when business was slow, and—"

Carly finished the sentence for her. "And business was slow more and more often, wasn't it? She was testing you. Couldn't believe you wouldn't ask for help. She'd have given you the shirt off her back."

"It was never more than a few dollars. A ten here, a twenty there. One time, a fifty I saw a customer give her. She didn't miss it. She didn't need it. But my shop was bleeding me dry. She knew I needed money. Why didn't she offer it? Isn't that what a genuine friend would do? But no. Not Rosella. With her, everything was business." She spat out the last word like it was a curse. "Sure, she offered me a loan. A loan? I couldn't pay back the money. I told her no thanks."

Grandma Carly motioned to Bernadette to sit, but the woman shook her head and crossed her arms over her chest. Her grandmother shrugged then turned back to the group. "Bernadette had the means. Her husband was a diabetic. A wig disguise. And she's the right height." She paced the small area rug and then paused. "But the cruelest cut of all was when Rosella told Bernadette she changed her will."

"She did—"

Grams whirled and strode to the tiny woman. "Yes, she did. Again, she made a note in her cash book. *Told Bernadette today she's gotten all she's going to get from me.*"

Detective Hogan stood. "Why couldn't it be Arthur? He's the shortest man, and Ginger's description could be off a few inches." He sat again. "Statistically speaking, it's usually family."

Arthur stood, pushing the chair back with the force of his motion, and glared at the police officer. Then he pivoted and pointed a finger at Bernadette. "You told me she wrote me out and put you in." Veins in his temples pulsed. "You tried to trick me into helping you."

Bernadette's hands clenched. "Shut up, you idiot."

Detective Hogan motioned for Arthur to sit. "Let's all stay calm, please."

Margie crossed to stand beside her grandmother. "One set of voices Aunt Rosella heard were you and Bernadette. Was she trying to convince you to help her?"

He shook his head and sat. "No. I was warning her off. Aunt

102

Rosella told me somebody was stealing, and she was convinced it was Bernadette. I figured if the old bat started looking into the books too closely, she'd see what I was up to, and then we'd both be in hot water."

The detective sneered. "Protecting your aunt's estate for your own benefit?"

"I wasn't getting anything from her. More than once after she changed the will she hinted that my share would be considerably smaller than I'd hoped for, because of shrinking inventory and cash losses. She knew what I was up to, and Bernadette, too. But I couldn't bring myself to say anything." He buried his face in his hands then looked up, eyes wet. "I wish now I had."

A commotion at the door, and Margie turned as Bernadette rushed through the opening, tripped on the top step, and fell into the arms of two waiting officers, her wig flying in the opposite direction.

A brief struggle, then the woman collapsed, sobbing and claiming her innocence, then turning the entire fault back on the dead woman. "If she hadn't told me about the will, I wouldn't have done it. But she gloated. She knew how much I needed the money. Instead, she told me not to come back to the store. Said she wouldn't have people around her that she didn't trust." Her twisted and tear-stained expression conveyed her true feelings. "Trust? What about our friendship? I hate her. I'm glad she's dead."

Grandma Carly stood on the step. "How did you convince her to let you in?"

"I told her I wanted to apologize. To pay back what I stole.

Asked if we could start again. She invited me in for coffee."

"How sad to abuse an opportunity for forgiveness and reconciliation so cruelly."

"Forgive? Reconcile?" The wig lady's face, mottled red, mascara running down her cheeks, shook her head. "Never."

The police officers got her back on her feet, handcuffed her, and led her away to their cruiser.

Before they tucked her into the back seat, Bernadette looked at the group gathered outside the store. "I didn't mean that. I'm sorry she's dead. I miss her so much. But I just couldn't fathom knowing I'd never be able to see her again. Never share a coffee or a meal or a joke. You understand why I had to do it, right?"

After the car pulled away, Grams stepped back inside and began clearing the coffee service.

Margie joined her, then wrapped an arm around her shoulders. "You are amazing. You prefer to be in the background." She gestured to the dirty cups and empty pot. "Doing this kind of thing. Yet you were born to do what you just did."

Her grandmother smiled, her cheeks pink. "Thank you. I really enjoyed this time, although I wish it were under different circumstances. But thanks to this mystery, now I have the ending of my novel figured out. I'll spend the rest of my vacation working on it, if you don't mind?"

"Not at all." Margie laughed. "And I'll spend the rest of my vacation working on the store. Reorganizing the books. Arranging titles by cover color doesn't help customers find what they're looking for."

"So you'll stay?"

Margie nodded. "I will. I'll take it one day at a time. See how I fit in. I'm definitely not as eclectic as Aunt Rosella. I'm sure that despite the mystery titles carried in my little shop, nothing this exciting will ever happen here again."

Her grandmother shook her head. "I've said that so many times when your grandfather and I were traveling for work. Or planning a wedding. '*What could possibly go wrong?*' I'd ask him. Well, he soon found out. And you will, too."

"Well, you're wrong. Sleepy little Edgewater is just the place I need after six years in college. A place to dip my feet into business, read as many books as I want, and live and work in the same place. What could go wrong?"

Thanks so much for reading this first installment of "Mysterious Ink Bookstore Mysteries".

I loved writing the "By the Numbers" series, featuring Carly Turnquist, forensic accountant, but last year, Carly told me *Risk Management*, which released in June 2020, would be her final book. I didn't want to say goodbye to her yet, and decided to offer my faithful readers an extra installment, one that introduced the new series yet assured readers that Carly was going to be fine.

If you enjoyed this book, I hope you'll leave a review online wherever you usually leave reviews.

If you'd like to journey with Margie, please check out the second book, "Little Grey Cells",
https://www.amazon.com/dp/B08KDNR5TF
and the rest of the series:
https://www.amazon.com/dp/B08KDNR5TF

About Leeann & Donna:

Leeann Betts, before she retired to a sunny and warm beach in 2019, wrote contemporary romantic suspense. Now, her real-life persona, Donna Schlachter, pens both contemporary and historical romantic suspense. Donna has published more than 60 novellas and full-length novels. They ghostwrite, judge writing contests, edit, facilitate a critique group, and are members of various writers groups. Donna travels extensively to research her stories, and is proud to be represented by Terrie Wolf of AKA Literary LLC, while Leeann relaxes as much as she can.

Keeping in Touch

Donna is taking all the information she's learned along the way about the writing and publishing process, and is coaching committed career writers. Learn more at https://www.donnaschlachter.com/the-purpose-full-writer-coaching-programs Check out her coaching group on FB: https://www.facebook.com/groups/604220861766651

www.DonnaSchlachter.com Stay connected so you learn about new releases, preorders, and presales, as well as check out featured authors, book reviews, and a little corner of peace. Plus: Receive 2 free ebooks simply for signing up for our free newsletter!

www.DonnaSchlachter.com/blog

Facebook: www.Facebook.com/DonnaschlachterAuthor

Twitter: www.Twitter.com/DonnaSchlachter

Books: Amazon: http://amzn.to/2ci5Xqq

Bookbub: https://www.bookbub.com/authors/donna-schlachter

Goodreads: https://www.goodreads.com/search?utf8=%E2%9C%93&query=donna+schlachter

The Purpose-Full Writer: https://www.facebook.com/groups/604220861766651

Need a writing coach? https://www.donnaschlachter.com/the-purpose-full-writer-coaching-programs